GW01401334

The Wishing Stone

Chronicles of Gam Gam Book Two
Adam Holcombe

BOUNTY
INK PRESS

Also by Adam Holcombe

Chronicles of Gam Gam

A Necromancer Called Gam Gam
The Wishing Stone

Bounty Inc

Bounty Inc (Coming 2025)

THE
WISHING
STONE

CHRONICLES OF GAM GAM
BOOK TWO

ADAM HOLCOMBE

BOUNTY
INK PRESS

First published by Bounty Ink Press 2024.

Cover Illustration by Kerstin Espinosa Rosero © 2024.

Cover Design by VM Designs © 2024.

Edited by Taya Latham.

Proofread by Isabelle Wagner at Emerald Scribe Proofreading.

Nugget's Tenth Life edited by Sue Bavey.

ISBN: 978-1-960544-04-9 (Paperback)

ISBN: 978-1-960544-05-6 (Hardcover)

BOUNTY
INK PRESS

bountyink.com

To Dylan.
Thanks for believing in my abilities
before reading a single word!

1

It's an incredible stench, that of two dead bodies locked in a wagon for any length of time. Rather hard to explain, like meat gone bad mixed with fruit gone bad mixed with a dirty diaper. Not something that was an issue on the road, where the undead could sit atop the wagon in the breeze. But within the city, Gam Gam was forced to keep them locked in, away from panicky people less used to walking corpses. Which is precisely why she had sought out the nearest charm stand and traded for two stink-free trinkets, giving up a freshly knit white cardigan with pink flowers and a matching hat.

The market was a busy place; it always was in Capital City, known for its people, its crowds, and its places for people to crowd. She didn't much care for it, but clients in search of a necromancer were rather rare and she had to make do. Especially with a young girl to feed and clothe.

The first five months had been a rush of adventure as Gam Gam had taken Mina sightseeing. They had raced south, away from the chilling winters, and swung back north just as the snow and ice had begun to melt. Not disappear, mind you, as there were still the occasional snowfalls. But now the day would heat up enough to turn it all to slush and make walking outdoors a nightmare without sturdy, waterproof boots.

The trip had been much needed for both to escape their lives, to heal and recover. But all vacations must come to an end and a growing child eats considerably more than an elderly woman. Coin was needed and that meant Gam Gam would need to take up a necromancy job. Or a real job, but she preferred the necromancy ones.

"Mina?" Gam Gam called out as she arrived back at the wagon. She had rented a space in the Stalls, typically reserved for traveling merchants to park their carts and wagons or even to sell straight from. For Gam Gam, she liked it because it was cheaper than the inns and it included a parking spot. She pet the two horses, Sebastian and Nora, her hand slipping through the illusion to run across the bone beneath, then she went around the side. "Mina?"

The rear doors were locked when Gam Gam tried them, so she rummaged through her purse for the key—which required little rummaging, really, as the purse had deflated since she had gone to the market. Several knitted goods had condensed into coin and a pair of charms no larger than a locket. A purse should never be so empty as this. She would need to restock it with more finished projects.

She pulled the doors open and the stench wafted out. Gam Gam went a bit green and choked down her gagging noises as she didn't want to be rude. Mina wouldn't be in there, that's for sure.

Sloughy and Gerald sat across from each other playing Cat's Cradle. A little more of Sloughy's fingers wore off with each passing of the string. He was becoming more bone by the day.

"Hello, dears. I bought you something." She smiled as she pulled herself into the wagon, careful to breathe as little as possible. Again, she rummaged through her purse, this time pulling out a small, wrapped package. Within were two oak crests, ribbons looped through a small hole in each to make a necklace. The undead reluctantly stopped their game to let her place the charms around each neck. Within moments, the air freshened to a tolerable level.

"Ah, that's better," Gam Gam said. She looked around the wagon and confirmed her earlier suspicion: Mina wasn't here. She wasn't the only one missing, however. "Nugget?"

Sloughy and Gerald stared at her with empty eyes.

"Do you know where they are?"

They shrugged.

Gam Gam sighed.

It wasn't the girl's first disappearance to explore the large city. It made Gam Gam nervous, but she refused to cage Mina. She just hoped Mina would stay safe.

"Gam Gam?"

Gam Gam turned and found a young man standing outside her wagon, familiar, with short copper hair, a crooked nose, and a large, toothy smile.

"Franky! I'll be right out."

Gam Gam climbed from the wagon, the last little hop down always sending an ache through her knees. She didn't let that stop her from grabbing Franky and giving him a big hug though.

"It's good to see you again too, Gam Gam," Franky laughed with his usual boisterous charm. She could feel the vibrations of his guffaw through their embrace.

Gam Gam pulled away and looked Franky in his mossy brown eyes. "How are your parents doing?"

"Oh, you know. Pa's still runnin' his shop, tellin' everyone else there they don't know how to do nuthin'. Askin' me back, though I told him that ain't me. Ma just got back from a trip with Aunt Karas."

"A good trip, I hope."

"For a while." Franky laughed. "The two were at each other's throats by the end though."

"Do you need new mittens?" Gam Gam indicated the man's bare hands with a glance. "I should have a pair around here somewhere."

"Oh, I have them right here." Franky pulled a pair from his pockets, a yellow and white mixture that reminded Gam

Gam of eggs. The young man seemed especially fond of them, however.

"You ought to be wearing those, Franky. You know how your hands get chapped if they're exposed to the cold too much."

"I do!" he said. "Well, mosta the time. Sometimes I need my fingers more free and other times I just don't wanna get them dirty, ya know?"

"That's what washing them is for. They're meant to get dirty."

Franky smiled and slipped them on. "Warm as the day you got 'em for me."

"Thanks for appeasing an old lady." Gam Gam smiled back. "Now what brings you this way?"

"Oh, heard you were in town and swung over. Clyde wanted me to drop some information off for you."

"Information?"

"Yeah, on that special case you have us looking into."

Gam Gam froze. She had nearly forgotten about *that*. The recent time spent with Mina had helped distract her from a lot of things. But if they had a lead, that could mean...

"What is the information?" Her voice was almost breathless, her mittened hands clutching at each other.

"Well, it might not be much, but he had a guy askin' around for some help, the kind a necromancer can do for him, and Clyde said he might know such a person. He asked what the man had to offer and the man said anything. Clyde says, 'What you mean, anything?' And it turns out the man meant nearly anything. He's a soldier, I guess, and not just that. He works the Eternal Emperor's own vaults more often than not. Said he could get anything the emperor kept there."

"It's not there, is it?" Gam Gam asked. "I asked around. My research says it can't be in the vaults."

"Oh no, it sure ain't. Clyde asked the fellow about glowing stones and his eyes narrowed and he got that dumb look on his face. There was no stone, he said, but he knew of a map."

"A map? What map?"

"A treasure map. As far as he could tell, a pretty useless one as it ain't led no one to treasure. But he says there's a glowing orb drawn in the corner. Some say that's the prize. He says he'll pay for your services with the map and a location."

"What location?"

"Well, seems the map is of a secret place and the location is how to get to the secret place."

"If the Eternal Emperor has a map to the Wishing Stone in his vaults, why hasn't he retrieved it?"

Franky shrugged at this. "I dunno, but what does the man who has everything need a wish for?"

"Maybe he doesn't, but he wouldn't want someone else's wish to ruin his perfect empire."

"Fair point. Clyde said somethin' similar. That's why I said it might not be much."

"Know what the soldier wants for a service?"

"No, but based on the hush hush of it, it ain't anything too big. Maybe just wants an undying pet." Franky looked around, then spotted Sloughy and Gerald and flashed them a smile they did not return. "Where is Little Nug anyway?"

"I don't know," Gam Gam admitted.

Franky's words flowed through her head without leaving much of a mark. Her focus had turned entirely to the map. She weighed the proposition in her head, the good and the bad, the risks and the dangers. It seemed a safe enough bet, though if this soldier got caught stealing, she would hate for it to trace back to her, or rather to Mina. Sergeant Mikyal may have lost his memories, but he would not be the only one after her; if her secret leaked, Mina would be in trouble again. Five months on the road hadn't been all for the sake of vacation. Gam Gam had watched and waited to see if anyone would chase them or try to find them. Coming back to the city these past four weeks had been a risk in itself; could she risk it further for a mere chance? She wondered what Mina would want and smiled, the answer already in her head. The girl was brash and bold; she would jump at the chance. And that meant Gam Gam should too.

"How soon can the meeting be set up?" Gam Gam asked.

"Oh, Clyde said whenever. Just need a few hours heads up to get a message to the man through the mimic stone. He got the map already, it sounds like, just waitin' for you."

"Wonderful. Could you do a favor for me, Franky? Could you get that set up for today?"

"Absolutely, Gam Gam. No problem on my end."

"Hang on. I'll get you a pair of socks for your troubles."

"Ain't no problem, Gam Gam, I got a pair right here." Franky lifted a pant leg to show off the raggedy sock beneath.

"Franky, dear, your socks are in terrible shape. How have you gone through them so quick?"

"Oh, it's what happens when ya wear 'em every day, no?"

"Every day? You don't switch socks?"

"Nope, I don't got any others to switch."

Gam Gam reached out with a thread of nauseating necromancy, that same sickly feeling rolling through her stomach every time she touched her magic. Gerald rose at its touch and searched through a chest, returning with five pairs of socks in hand. Gam Gam took them and proffered them to Franky. "I won't take no for an answer. Wearing the same pair every day can't be good for your feet. Take them and remember to swap between them. And wash them occasionally."

"Oh, thank you very much, Gam Gam." Franky grabbed the bundle of socks and put them in a pocket. "I'll switch 'em when I'm done talking to Clyde."

"Thank you, dear."

"I better get going if you want that meeting."

"Stay safe, Franky. Don't get into any trouble."

"I tend to, Gam Gam. Problem is, trouble always comes looking." Franky guffawed as he waved farewell and Gam Gam smiled as he left.

"Now," Gam Gam said, turning to the two undead loitering in her wagon, "where are Mina and Nugget?"

2

M ina weaved through the crowd, silent as a specter, bare feet brushing across rough stone. It had been flat once, long ago, before the wind and the rain had etched a thousand stories into its skin, when the stone elemancers had first raised the great stone apartments from the ground and stacked them one atop the other. She slipped from the crowd onto the third story terrace overlooking the market square. She paused to bring her breathing under control as she crept down the alley and peered out at the balcony beyond.

A boy, two years older than Mina, sat on the edge, feet kicking the open air as he ate a sandwich that was likely stolen. Mina smiled, taking a careful stop forward to—

Her hands flew to her mouth, stopping just in time before they could slap against her lips and alert the boy. A scream died in her mouth before it could live to give her away. She bit her lip and urged the tears away. She pulled her foot back and found a jagged stone in her path, nearly the culprit of destroying her stealth. A hot pain pulsed against the otherwise cold numbness in her foot, but a few tentative steps proved she was not harmed. She glared at the evil stone, then her expression changed to thoughtfulness. A new idea. A smirk.

The boy continued eating his sandwich, unaware of all that had happened. Mina ducked and grabbed the pointy stone, warming it in her palm, the rough edges scratching against her fingers. She closed her eyes, took a deep breath, and pulled on her neuromancy.

Heat flooded her veins, muscles vibrating with a desire to do something. *Anything*. She wanted to move, to run around with the energy pulsing through her. She forced herself still and pushed out. A multitude of minds from among the crowd behind her exploded into her presence, flashing red and gold with the busy thoughts of those on the move, destinations to reach and tasks to perform. The boy's mind was a calm blue sea, contemplative but unhurried. Mina reached out with her presence, brushing against his consciousness and delving into his mind.

Through the fall and winter, Gam Gam had helped Mina practice her powers, not just hide them. She practiced concealing her presence when she used them so it couldn't be detected. She toyed with new tricks, some Gam Gam had come up with despite not being a neuromancer. One of these tricks she called a direct probe. Instead of providing prompts for memories, Mina could view the memories as they were being made. A form of viewing what was being thought about in that moment.

She felt herself at the pond of the boy's memories, the water of his mind waiting for something to stir into the depths. Mina pushed out with a concept in her mind rather than a prompt of words. She wanted *now*, but not as a memory. She wanted what happened now. Like petals floating up from the pond, the thoughts appeared, though only briefly before popping and disappearing. They were fleeting, unlike memories centering around a certain subject, and it required Mina to move quickly. She reached out for a petal as it appeared, pushing a small amount of her presence into it. The image of a young woman, no more than twice her age. Auburn hair, pale skin, moss-colored eyes. Freckles painted a constellation across her cheeks. She was pretty and comforting, though Mina was not sure if that was her analysis or the boy's thoughts. Or a mixture. Perhaps a crush of his?

Tell of a devil and summon it you shall.

Mina siphoned a copy of the memory and pushed out with her power, something which had become easier with practice. Instead of casting images from the memories, she could isolate certain parts, projecting only those she wanted and in a manner she chose. She could even manipulate them to some degree.

An illusion mimicking the boy's mysterious woman appeared near the next alley on the opposite side of the building. A long white gown flowed down her body, hiding the fact that Mina would cause it to glide rather than walk.

She stepped from her hiding place and threw the jagged stone at the feet of her illusion. Then, as she jumped back into the alley, she moved the illusion to do the same.

She watched as the boy jumped and turned, the sandwich disappearing into the folds of his cloak. Mina's tether to his mind wobbled as her concentration dipped. Anxiety and nerves pulsed through her, readying her. But still the illusion moved, the boy's eyes catching a glimpse as it disappeared into the crowd to the loud yells of several passersby.

The boy ran and Mina gave chase, creeping out only when her sightline was blocked. She spun around the next corner, hands outstretched, ready to grab him, and—

The boy ducked her grasp, facing her at the alley's opening. In a quick movement, his hand clutched hers and spun it around her back. He slammed her against the building and a grunt popped out of her mouth. Then the blade of a knife was to her neck and she squeaked to her dismay. Her cheeks flushed with embarrassment, compounded by the boy's laughter.

He dropped the knife and released her arm, still laughing. Mina spun and pushed him away. He was lithe and skinny, whereas Mina was stocky. He took the push and fell to his rump, though that did not stop his giggling.

"You could have hurt me, jerk!" She yelled the accusation, only to notice the knife had never left its sheath.

He grinned at her and tapped the sheath's point against his palm. "I've never seen a sheath hurt anybody before." Emil pocketed the blade and replaced it with the remains of his sandwich. Before taking a bite, he crooked an eyebrow and offered it to her. Mina glared, then sighed and shook her head.

It had taken almost a week before Gam Gam had let Mina wander the city alone—or as alone as Gam Gam would let her, though Mina enjoyed trying to lose Nugget in the crowds—and only a few days after that before she'd seen Emil for the first time. He had stolen fruit from a vendor and fled the chasing guards using Mina as a distraction. He had snuck up on her afterward and surprised her with one of the fruits. A peace offering, he had said. She had seen him nearly every day since, at least when Gam Gam hadn't needed her around.

Emil returned to his perch at the terrace's edge and Mina sidled up next to him. People filled the market square, stopping between shops and booths, like a thousand beetles scurrying to find their next food. Capital City sprouted out around them in twisting alleys and towering buildings. It wasn't anything like Mina's village. It was so much larger in every direction. The city spread out farther, grew taller, and dug deeper. The people were alien as well, always so busy and focused, like everything they did had immense purpose behind it. It gave Mina headaches to delve into their minds. She had hated the city before Emil had taught her to find the quiet spots. To watch the people and how they moved. To let her mind relax despite the stress that flowed around her.

She turned to her friend, face cooled from the earlier embarrassment, and finally asked her question. "How'd you know it was me this time?"

"Big tip for you," Emil said around a mouthful of sandwich. "Don't use a dead girl to catch my attention. It's a dead giveaway." Then he laughed and swallowed the food. "Get it, dead giveaway."

Mina felt her gut clench and guilt wash over her in waves. Her hand hovered up to her chest, where beneath her clothing a pair of rings dangled near her heart. "That wasn't your sister, was it?" She winced as she looked at Emil's face. His hair was darker and freckles sparser, but she could see the similarities. The eyes were different though. His were dark brown. The kind of eyes to sink into and escape from the world.

Emil chewed the last of his sandwich, stretching the silence for as long as he could. He swallowed and turned to her, a strange seriousness stretching across his face. "Yes, it was." His words like nails hammered into her. Then he leaned forward, nose scrunched. "But I'll forgive you if you give me some cookies."

Mina's brows furrowed. "Wait, how'd you know?"

He smiled, bright and inviting, the same as his sister's smile. "I can smell 'em. Hand 'em over!"

Mina's guilt cracked beneath Emil's kindness and she smiled back. From her pocket, she pulled the linen-wrapped bundle and handed it over. Emil readily grabbed it and tore into the package, lifting a smooshed, gooey cookie into the air. A piece broke off and tumbled back onto the linen with the other cookies.

"Next time let me know before I throw you against the wall that you're bringing cookies." He smiled at the mess of smashed cookies and ate the piece he still held. He let out a great sigh and said, "Gods, they're still so soft and gooey! They're best like that. Have I ever told you Gam Gam makes the best cookies?"

"Many times. That's why I keep bringing them."

"Good, don't stop. I'm ending this friendship if you ever stop bringing them."

Mina giggled at the false threat and rubbed her sweaty palms against her knees. Winter was thawing, but it wasn't warm enough that she should be this sweaty. And she *definitely* wasn't nervous! What would she even be nervous about? Possibly losing her only friend forever? Because that wasn't going to happen. Right?

"So, um…" Mina started, then fizzled out as the words failed to come.

Emil looked over, eyebrow crooked, and held out a mangled treat. "Cookie?"

Mina laughed. "I've already had several." He shrugged and shoved the whole thing into his mouth. Mina continued, "But there's an easier way to get cookies, you know."

"I told you," he said around a mouthful of cookie, "none of the bakeries around here are as good. And the only cookies easy to steal are a day old and a crumbly mess."

"No, I mean Gam Gam's cookies. You know she'd be fine if you came with us. You could have a home, meals you don't have to steal. You might have to do a few chores like I do, but they're not too bad. And with both of us doing them, it'd be even easier. But at least you wouldn't have to skulk around this city and steal to live."

Emil's chewing slowed as he stared out at the city below him, watching the people scurrying about. Mina resisted reaching into his mind to see what he was thinking. Instead, she shrugged and added, "Plus, then we could hang out more, not just when I'm in Capital City."

"I have a home, Mina." His arms spread out and his sullen face shifted into the mask of a smile. "The city is my home. I wouldn't know what to do with all those rules and strictness."

"Gam Gam's not strict."

"But she's not this free either." He flashed a toothy grin. "What would she say if I stole some fruit from that stand over there?"

"She wouldn't be happy, but neither are the guards! So, you still live by rules."

He waved a hand in dismissal. "Guards are just around to scare off the cowards and catch the slow. It's fun once the guards get involved."

"And what happens when you get caught?"

"I never get caught."

Mina huffed in frustration. She wanted to convince Emil to come with them, not just for his own safety, but also because she would miss him when they left. Gam Gam talked about leaving the city soon and when they left, Mina would abandon her best friend. Her *only* friend. Something she hadn't had since her father's death.

But all her words scattered from her mind when the nearby bell tower rang out to mark the hour. Her eyes flared and she jumped to her feet.

"Oh no, I'm late!"

"See," Emil said. "Strict."

"No." Mina glared at the boy, hands on her hips. "It's not that. She's going to look for necromancy work and I was going to tag along to learn about it."

"But you're not a necromancer. You can't even openly use your magic."

"Maybe not right now." She shrugged. "But that doesn't mean we won't find somewhere I'm able." She glanced over at the tower as the bell finished ringing, then back at her friend. "Think about what I said. You can just come with us for a little bit. It doesn't have to be forever. Think of it like a vacation!"

She turned and ran to the alley's opening when Emil's words halted her. "Wait, Mina!" He stood and ran over to her, his dark eyes focusing on her own. "Be careful about any client Gam Gam finds. Anyone who needs a necromancer's help is bad news."

"I needed a necromancer's help."

"I think that proves my point," Emil said with a big smile. Mina glared and playfully pushed him away, then ran into the crowds of the street, his laughter chasing her.

Mina navigated the crowd again, ducking under a large wooden bench carried by two men and slipping around a horse led by a family, its saddle bags stuffed with groceries. She retraced her steps through the slithering side roads until she arrived at the market square she had looked down on not so long ago. She looked up at the third terrace, to her friend, and waved at the small speck that stood at the balcony's edge, looking down onto the world.

When she turned away, the market crowd consumed her like a fresh batch of cookies, pulling her into its depths until the sound of bartering came from everywhere at once. She yelled out multiple times as boots nicked her still bare feet, but the offenders never took notice. She pushed her way through until she burst out on the other side, near the Stalls.

By the time Mina spotted Gam Gam's wagon, she was covered in a sheen of sweat and breathing heavily. All numbness fled from her hands and feet as the high sun brought a warmth to wake the world.

Mina sprinted the last bit, bouncing off a wayward customer with a shouted apology. She stopped by Sebastian and Nora, giving the undead horses each a pet. Cloaked in their illusory guises, they did not respond to the touch. Mina didn't mind if they were just puppets; their presence was still comforting. A reminder of a time when she had felt strong riding atop Sebastian.

Mina ran around the side of the wagon and slid to a halt as she came face to face with Gam Gam. "Oh, you're back!" she gasped between breaths. "I was just out for a, um, run..."

"A run to meet Emil?" Gam Gam quirked an eyebrow, a hint of a smile on her lips.

Mina's eyes widened. How had she known? It was as if Gam Gam had used neuromancy on her and the thought made her uncomfortable. Which made her more uncomfortable with her own powers. She shook it off and barreled on. "He's a good person, Gam Gam! I promise. He's just had it difficult living on his own, is all."

The hint turned into a full smile and Gam Gam leaned forward, placing a hand on Mina's shoulder. With Mina's latest growth spurt, the necromancer needed less leaning these days. "I'm not worried about the boy, dear. I trust your judgment given your situation." Gam Gam put emphasis on the words, careful not to be too loud. In a quieter voice, she added, "It's using your powers that worries me. We're in the heart of the Eternal Empire now and if anyone finds out..."

Surprise widened Mina's eyes, laying the truth of Gam Gam's statement bare. "But... I... It was..." Mina's mouth flailed for a defense, but she had none. She had used her powers to try to win a stupid game. "How did you know?"

As if to answer her question, a skeletal cat squeezed through the crowd and plodded up next to her, stretching. She could almost see the wink as he looked up at her with his empty eye sockets.

"Nugget!" Mina kicked at the undead cat, who was far too quick and dodged her easily. Mina wobbled unsteadily as Nugget circled to Gam Gam's side and stared at her.

"Where are your shoes?!" Gam Gam looked down at Mina's feet in shock. Mina followed her gaze and noticed the dirt caked across the sides of her feet. She felt her face burning.

"I'm quieter without them," she said.

"Quieter? Why do you need to be quieter?"

"Emil and I have this game where I try to sneak up on him." Mina shrugged. "I haven't won yet and thought it might help me."

"And that is why you used your powers? To help you win this game?"

"Yes, but he already knew about them. I trust him. He wouldn't turn on me." In a whisper, she continued, "He lost his sister to the empire. He wouldn't turn on me."

"What if someone else saw you use them? Or heard you discussing them? What if a neuromancer got a hold of your friend and found out anyway?"

Mina looked away from the questions, each delivering a sting as strong as any whip, though these found her heart instead of her skin.

Gam Gam sighed and put her hands on Mina's shoulders. "Mina." She paused. "Just because we've dealt with Mikyal doesn't mean there aren't others out there who would want to use you for their personal gain or to win favor with the empire. You know the emperor has put out a call for neuromancers. If the guards caught you—"

"They won't!" Mina raised her head in defiance and Gam Gam's eyebrows rose. "Emil's the best at avoiding guards and he would never let me get caught."

"That's more worrisome than comforting, dear." Gam Gam smiled, which disappeared with a deep breath. "When it's due to theft, I'm sure he's wonderful at avoiding them. But this would be far more important to the guards and their emperor. I helped you with your powers so you could control them and protect yourself. Not to win competitions with friends."

Mina bowed her head. "I'm sorry, Gam Gam. I won't do it again."

Gam Gam's hand brushed across her cheek and Mina looked at her as guilt ate away at the lining of her stomach. "There will come a day, dear, where you won't have to hide so carefully."

"How do you know that?" Mina's stomach curdled, changing the guilt to annoyance. "As long as the Eternal Empire wants my kind, I'll have to stay hidden."

"There's no telling how long it will be around. Or maybe the call for neuromancers will end. Change is always lurking around every corner, be it good or bad. The future is forever in flux."

But all Mina could think of was Emil's freedom and she wondered what it would be like to be without restrictions. Was there a way to live freely as herself? To not have to hide who she was?

"Luckily, I found us a client," Gam Gam said, dropping her hand from Mina's shoulder as she shifted the conversation. "We have plenty of time before the meeting. Put some shoes on before your toes freeze off and we'll head out."

"You found a client?" Mina perked up, her guilt softly being brushed under the rug.

"Not just that," Gam Gam said with a big grin. "I also found some stink-free charms. Go on, take a whiff of the wagon. It smells as fresh as the day I bought it."

Mina smiled. That would be a nice change of pace. "So, where are we meeting your client?"

Gam Gam returned to the rear of the wagon and grabbed her bulging purse. "At the Dripping Bucket."

3

The name 'The Dripping Bucket' brought to mind several images, none of which impressed or excited Mina. Rundown, broken, makeshift. All around terrible. Traffic grew sparse as they drew close, the people looking sketchier and harsher with each step. Mina pulled closer to Gam Gam, though the old woman seemed unbothered by the rougher crowd. Mina wondered about the clientele of a place like the Dripping Bucket. She wondered if these were the people who prowled the outskirts and if they would get worse as they strode further in. A haven for the crooked and the broken.

As much as Mina prepared herself for the worst, the Dripping Bucket superseded all expectations.

Its sign dangled at an odd angle, threatening to drop on the next patron every time the door was forced open or closed. The door had to be forced as it didn't fit its frame, wedging firmly whenever it was closed against the cold air outside. A burly woman forced the door open, slamming it against the outside wall of the tavern, then entered. Gam

Gam rushed to follow, muttering about the sticky door being tricky.

Within, the floors were dirt and Mina was not entirely unconvinced the bar and tables weren't. The wood under the grime was scarred from decades of use and neglect; the only thing stopping the tables from wobbling was the legs being sunken into the dirt floor. The chairs, which didn't have the luxury of sitting in one place long enough to embed into the ground, wobbled with their inhabitants. A sweaty man tended the bar, wiping his face with the same rag with which he cleaned glasses. Which was the same rag he used on the bartop.

Mina could have overlooked the grime and the hole in the wall that was patched by a single board a third as wide. She could have ignored the rats that feasted on food droppings and ran along the rafters. But she had a difficult time ignoring the people.

As the door slammed against its frame and Gam Gam struggled to close it completely, every eye turned to them and silence descended. Mina felt her insides twist and her blood ran cold. Her hands turned numb as she looked at each staring gaze. Every new person was scarier than the last. Tougher, more muscular, more menacing. And each looked to be dealing with a sharper and larger stone in their shoe than their neighbors. Her eyes lingered on a strange trio in the corner.

The first man was overweight, shirtless, and had a long beard dyed pink and tied into a strange braid. He sat atop a second, much smaller and thinner man with bulging eyes, a sopping wet face, and an unusual haircut where the sides were shaved. The bulging eyes were caused by the first man, but the sopping wet face came from the woman who had taken a brief pause from pouring her beer onto his face. She was even scrawnier than the squished man, drowning in a massive dress with its hem tied up around her. She could have fit a dozen of her inside the dress and still had room to move.

The squished man was the last to turn his fading attention to Mina and even he raised an eyebrow at her arrival. As if her being here made even less sense than his own.

Why had Gam Gam agreed to meet someone here of all places? Mina's breath came in quick, short bursts, her lungs seemingly unable to hold as much air as normal. There was no way they were going to leave here alive, especially without Sloughy or Gerald. Mina had never wanted to be near a corpse quite so badly.

Well, okay, there was the one time. But *besides* that, she couldn't think of another case.

"Ah, got it," Gam Gam huffed as the door jammed shut again. She sighed and turned around next to Mina. She smiled as she surveyed the crowd.

A man rose from his seat at the bar, so tall his head nearly collided with the low beam, so wide his arms collided with everyone he passed. Shouts and curses chased him. His bald head was adorned with two long scars intersecting over a missing eye. A red blotch of skin crawled up one side of his neck as tattoos curled down the other side and across his arms. When he smiled, several of his teeth were shown to have vacated his mouth at some point in the past. Mina supposed she didn't need to consider why. He stopped in front of Gam Gam, crouching down to meet her gaze.

"Now, what do we have here?" he growled.

Mina clutched Gam Gam's hand and prayed the necromancer hadn't shut the door fully. But Gam Gam did not look ready to leave. Instead, she beamed at the giant hulking in front of her and said, "You've lost another tooth since I last saw you, Clyde. Have you been brushing like I told you?"

Clyde bellowed a laugh that shook Mina, then wrapped Gam Gam in a deadly embrace, except that Gam Gam's laughter echoed from somewhere within the tangle of muscle around her.

"I can't help it," Clyde said, releasing Gam Gam. "That paste tastes disgusting. If they made it ale flavored, maybe I'd do it every day."

"How are Shae and Lainie?"

"As wonderful as ever. Lainie hasn't stopped wearing that scarf you made her. Even inside. I have no idea how you make your stuff so soft."

"I have my sources." Gam Gam winked, then dug into her purse. "But that reminds me, I hope she enjoys a matching set." Gam Gam handed over a pair of mittens. Clyde's eyes widened and if Mina hadn't been scared out of her wits, she would have said they even grew watery.

Massive hands swallowed the mittens as he said, "You're too kind, Gam Gam!"

"Nonsense, it's my pleasure."

"Who's the little one?" Clyde asked as he pocketed the mittens, turning his one pale yellow eye to Mina. She stood statue-still under his gaze, worried a single movement or errant breath would break the strange quiet of the bar. Would remove her from this moment where there might be peace and shatter the tavern into chaos. And so, she returned his gaze with her own wide-eyed stare, mouth agape. Little did she realize that the bar had returned to its general chaos and disorder, having withdrawn their notice of the new entrants.

"This is Mina." Gam Gam put a hand on Mina's shoulder for emphasis or perhaps comfort. "She came under my care recently and I'm showing her the ropes of being a mage."

Clyde grunted and looked over his shoulder. "Speaking of which, that's your client over there." He emphasized a table where a man stood straight and stared at Gam Gam. "Been nursing an ale for twenty minutes, trying his best to ignore everyone. He rushed down here once I sent him the message."

"Thank you for setting everything up, Clyde. I'll be sure to make the meeting quick, so he doesn't disturb the pub for much longer. Or more likely, the reverse."

"I think the others are having a good time with it." Clyde chuckled. "Every time Lyla pours another beer on that poor oaf, your client's veins pop out a little more."

While speaking, Clyde dug around in another pocket and pulled something small and shiny from within. Then he knelt in front of Mina, holding the jagged stone in front of him. It looked like a pebble in his hands. He gestured to the slightly blue, slightly transparent crystal and said in a low voice, smoothing the edges of his normally gruff tone, "Luxore is a strange gem. When exposed to darkness, it creates its own light." He wrapped his other palm around the one holding the gem and held it tightly closed for a few seconds. Then he cracked open a space between thumb and palm. A faint blue light glowed from within.

He opened his hand fully and the glow died away nearly as fast. The gesture pulled her attention away from the other patrons, who she now noticed had returned to their conversations and waterboarding. The anxiety leaked from her body, breaths came easier, sensation returned to her fingers. She smiled at Clyde, thankful for the gesture, but found his focus still on the gem. He brought one finger down on it and the stone turned to a paste that spread across his palm. He molded the paste with a single finger until a smooth, unbroken ring sat in the center of his hand.

He held the gorgeous ring between forefinger and thumb, and with his other hand, he gently grabbed Mina's, pulling it toward him. He slid the ring onto Mina's index finger. "A perfect fit. When the darkness is the worst, remember that you can create your own light."

With a grunt, he stood back up and spoke at his normal volume with a great shrug. "My daughter loves hers. If you don't like it, you can always toss it away. Luxore is cheap. Just try not to do it while I'm looking." He bellowed another boisterous laugh and settled a palm on Gam Gam's shoulder. "It's good to see you again Gam Gam and I'm glad to have met you, Mina."

Mina smiled at her ring. She was covering it with one hand to try to produce the glow but couldn't figure out how to block all the light from reaching it. It was only when Gam Gam nudged her that she remembered to thank Clyde for the gift.

"It was good to see you too, Clyde." Gam Gam patted his arm and the giant returned to his seat with another round of shouts and curses and, in one case, a half-empty bowl of peanuts being tossed at him. The peanut dish was returned with more force, knocking the original tosser to the ground with a large lump forming above one eye.

Mina spun around to the sounds of a great crash and clatter. A new guest had pulled the door open too hard, slamming it into the wall and causing the sign to break loose. He now lay on the ground, limp, with the Dripping Bucket's sign atop him. There was a short silence, then a great roar as the clientele jumped from seats and cheered. Two people hoisted the unconscious man up and waved his limp arms around in mock celebration.

"Free round for everyone," the bartender called out to another round of cheering.

Shouts of "Sign beer! Sign beer! Sign beer!" echoed around the bar.

"Shall we meet our client?" Gam Gam asked Mina. Distracted by the chaos of celebration, she only nodded in response.

The necromancer threaded her way between the cramped tables, stopping at each one to say hello and share pleasantries with more of the roughest looking people Mina had ever met. Each one burst into a smile and thanked her profusely for the gifts she pulled from her purse. Gam Gam asked about parents and siblings, significant others and children, pets and... Well, Mina wasn't entirely sure what one of the things she asked after was. She had no idea how Gam Gam had met all of these people, not without some strange and dark past, though no one here would have been old enough for that. Still, her anxiety melted away like the snow at winter's end, each new conversation displaying to Mina that these people were just people. Strange and harsh as they might look, each conversation showed a normal person beneath. She became more comfortable and said hello as she was introduced to a few of them.

"Sorry about that," Gam Gam said as she slid into the booth opposite her client. Mina slid in next to her. "A few friends happened to be here."

"A strange place to have friends," the client murmured, eyes shifting over to the man yelling for mercy between facefuls of ale. His two torturers released him and began celebrating.

Gam Gam leaned over and whispered, "Don't worry about them. It's a little game they like to put on to unnerve new guests."

The client glanced over, clearly straining to hear Gam Gam's words. He had short, blond hair draped down to just above his sapphire eyes. His jaw looked strong enough to crack walnuts against, with broad shoulders poking out from under his cloak.

"I used to frequent this pub in my college days," Gam Gam told the client.

"None of your *friends* seem old enough to have gone to college with you," he said. Then after a pause and a glance sideways, he added, "No offense, ma'am."

"None taken. I know how old I am. You requested the aid of a necromancer. How may I help you?"

"Yes, I talked to some colleagues and they mentioned a necromancer should be able to help." The client fidgeted in the pocket of his cloak but didn't withdraw what was in it.

"My brother's unit dispatched to a settlement on the coasts and it was a long journey. Some bandits or malcontents hit the unit, expecting a score. All they found was death. But so did my brother. The captain of the unit doesn't know where his remains were buried. It was a long, winding journey and he's prone to drinking his memories away. The others in the unit aren't certain either or they don't care enough to tell me. I would like to know where he was buried so I can bring his remains home to bury properly."

A soldier. Mina now spotted the two white circles on his breast poking out from beneath his cloak. The sigil of the Eternal Empire. Her heart thundered in her head and sweat seeped from her temples and palms. Trying to be discreet, she wiped her hands on her pants, but the nervous sweat returned within moments. The client glanced at her once, but his focus remained primarily on Gam Gam. Mina tried to sink into the bench, as far away from the soldier as she could get. To disappear from his view entirely. She looked down at her hands and noticed the blue ring. She twisted it with her other hand, focusing on the feel as the smooth gem rubbed against her finger. Letting the methodical motions pull her mind away from the moment.

"Do you have something of his?" Gam Gam asked. "The more important, the better. I can use it as a medium to commune, which should help me locate the remains."

The soldier nodded, finally removing his hand from his pocket. He set a small cloth bundle on the table between them. Gam Gam grabbed it and opened it.

"It was his favorite," the client said. "Wrote all his letters with it."

The necromancer inspected the pen, holding it up in the dim light, seeming to see something no one else could. Then she closed her eyes. Mina felt a faint stickiness in the air, like spilled honey on her skin. That meant Gam Gam was using her necromancy. It wasn't often that Mina could feel it, but having been around the necromancer so long, she could occasionally sense the magic's use like a change in the air around her.

"This should work. Do you have a map I can use?"

He nodded, removing a bundle of paper from another pocket and spreading the well-creased map out on the table.

"This will take a few minutes," Gam Gam said and, without waiting, she pointed the capped pen down on Capital City on the map. Her eyes filled with a dark purple glow and she stared off into the distance, her hand moving slowly across the map, occasionally causing a scratching sound as the pen scraped the paper.

Mina watched her for a few seconds, then grew bored. She glanced at the soldier and caught him glancing at her. Both looked away, then repeated the process. The awkwardness culminated until it turned stickier than Gam Gam's necromancy.

"So…" All thoughts fled Mina, so she fell back to the only thing she could think of to say. "What do you do?"

"I'm a soldier in the emperor's army," he said, clearly unwilling to share more than that.

"Cool." Mina looked across the room and watched Clyde laughing with the dazed, sign-felled man who now had several different glasses in front of him. The scrawny woman who had been pouring beer was at his other shoulder, swinging her arms in wild gestures as she told a story.

"So, what are you?" the soldier asked, bringing Mina's attention back to him. "A little necromancer?"

Mina smiled, stifling a laugh. "Kinda."

"Have you seen undead?"

"Yeah."

"Are they as violent as they say?"

Mina shrugged. "How violent do they say they are?"

"I have some friends who talked of an undead outbreak in a town not too long ago. Out in the countryside. They claim an army stormed through the city and tore apart the inn, attacked their entire unit." He leaned forward conspiratorially as he continued. "They claim they faced an entire horde, slayed them all, but no casualties on their end. No one was even bitten. And you know what happens when you're bitten, I'm sure."

Mina shook her head, eyes wide in panic, though she hoped the soldier would think she was just scared of his story.

"They turn you," he continued. "You become an undead and pass the curse on. Thing is, their sergeant remembers nothing and never reported the undead. Not to mention they were never supposed to be out that way anyway. Bunch of liars is what they are." He shrugged, then seemed to think about it more. "Not sure why the sergeant took them there against orders. He never said. Then had some kind of stroke or something and claimed he couldn't remember why."

Mina wanted to reach inside the soldier's head and tear out every memory of herself. Her hands shook and she kept glancing at Gam Gam, hoping for a swift finish to the commune. Blood drained from Mina's face and the soldier's brow furrowed in concern.

"Are you all right?" he asked. "Didn't mean to scare you. I'm sure your grandma's undead are under much better control. Whole thing reeks of lies anyway."

Mina nodded, but her dry mouth refused to allow her words. The client was about to speak again when Gam Gam spoke.

"Finished." Her hand paused over an area to the south of Capital City, angled to the east a tad. "He was heading south and they shifted to the east. Bad weather, maybe, it wasn't clear. There is a barn here, with green and red stripes. Beyond that a small copse. He and three others were buried at the base of the trees there. Shouldn't be hard to find. Someone took time to etch their names into the trees."

The soldier's eyes brightened. "You really found him?"

"Yes," Gam Gam said. "The pen's pull was strong. I am certain of his location. I am sorry for your loss, but I hope this helps with your closure."

The soldier took the pen back, taking a moment to mark the spot on the map before rolling it back in its cloth. He returned the pen and map to his pockets and pulled free another piece of paper.

"I'll be sure to head there next leave. Thank you for your help, necromancer." He slid the paper over and Gam Gam took it. Her other hand grabbed the soldier's and he looked at her.

"How do I know that no one will wonder where this came from?"

"Because it disappears all the time," he answered gruffly. "It's a right of passage for new soldiers to sneak it from the vault and go on a hunt. No one will think anything of it going missing for good. But there's nothing down there. It's probably not even real. If it was, the Eternal Emperor himself would have retrieved it by now." Then the soldier rose from his seat and departed from the pub as quickly as he could to the jeers of several patrons.

The necromancer opened the paper carefully as though it might crumble to dust. Another, smaller piece fell loose and opened on the table, appearing to be a detailed note. The paper in Gam Gam's hands was a map, though Mina couldn't tell what it could be a map of. It seemed to be several interlocking areas creating a map with large open spots.

"What is that?" Mina asked.

"A map to something very important." She tucked the note into the map and placed both in her purse.

"A map of where?"

"The catacombs deep under the city." Then she glanced at Mina with a smile. "Good thing you have your new ring to light our way."

4

"We'll swing by the wagon first," Gam Gam said as she pushed her shoulder into the door, wood squealing against wood as it slowly opened. They stepped over the broken sign and into the alley. "There are some supplies that will help us."

"Are we bringing Gerald and Slou—oof!"

Mina rebounded off a short, cloaked man rushing toward the tavern. "Mina?" he said, lowering his hood.

"Emil?" She blinked several times to be sure of what she saw. Why was her friend in such a hurry to get to the tavern? "What are you doing here?"

His cheeks burned red and his gaze darted away from hers. "I'm looking for you."

"Why?"

"I watched you leave the market square and traced you heading this way. Only thing over here is the Dripping Bucket. Do you have any idea the kind of scoundrels that frequent this place? Even I wouldn't step inside there." He paused and rubbed the back of his neck, some tension leaving his shoulders. "I mean, I was going to, in order to save you. But I wouldn't enter by my choice."

"Many of those scoundrels are my friends," Gam Gam said, flashing a smile to ease the jest. "They look less scoundrelly once you get to know them."

"Oh! I didn't mean anything by calling them... um... scoundrels," Emil finished flatly, unwilling to meet anyone's gaze.

"So, you're Emil, I take it?" Gam Gam drew his attention back and he nodded quickly. "It's nice to finally meet you. Mina's talked a lot about you."

Emil stared at the outstretched hand, then jerked his own forward and shook it. "Uh, you too, Gam Gam, ma'am."

"We're exploring the catacombs if you want to come," Mina chimed in.

"Mina, quiet," Gam Gam whispered and shot her a severe look.

"The catacombs?" Emil asked. "Why?"

"Shh!" Gam Gam shushed.

"Yeah, we're looking for—"

"Mina, enough!" Mina fell silent at Gam Gam's expression. The necromancer grabbed each of their arms and pulled them on. "We can speak more at the wagon, but not out where anyone can listen."

"Okay." The kids spoke in unison, then looked at each other. Though the severity of Gam Gam's voice had been intended to impress upon them the dangers of what they were doing, Mina and Emil only saw adventure and excitement. Both smiled, eyes shining.

Gam Gam released them as they merged into the crowded market square and pushed their way to the Stalls.

"Is it okay if Emil comes?" Mina asked as Gam Gam unlocked the doors.

"If he wishes." She climbed inside and pulled open a few drawers and chests, above which hung three alabaster-white rectangles, the likenesses of four individuals raised against them in perfect detail. Mina knew them well, as she had made them herself—the one of Gam Gam's grandkids so long ago on the cliffside and the ones of her daughter and son-in-law at a later time as Mina had practiced her abilities. Mina had hoped to add a fourth up there, but she hadn't been able to pull her own memories forward in the same way.

Gam Gam returned with Sloughy and Gerald following, Nugget curled on Sloughy's shoulders. They held five readied lanterns between them, with Nugget accounting for none. Gam Gam pulled out a large bag that clinked like dice and stuck it into her bulging purse, reluctantly pulling a cowl out to make room. "There shouldn't be any danger. The catacombs were sealed long ago. Anything down there will be dead or undead, and undead happens to be my specialty."

"Then why did we have to be quiet?"

"I don't wish to turn our adventure into a competition," Gam Gam said with a conspiratorial smile. It shifted to a frown though as she added, "Nor would we want any soldiers to think we're up to anything worth investigating." She gave Mina a knowing stare, who averted her eyes.

"We're bringing Gerald and Sloughy?" Mina looked at the pair of undead and their many lanterns.

"I think they will be of good help to us." Gam Gam non-verbally communicated with the undead and they handed a lantern off to each of the kids. Emil took his hesitantly. "And extra hands are always useful. Is there anything the two of you would like before we depart? A cookie perhaps?"

"No, thank you, Gam Gam," Emil said, looking a little green. "I already had one or two."

"One or two?" Mina asked as she eyed his queasy look. "Did you eat them *all*?"

"They were tasty." Emil held a hand to his stomach and sighed. "I regret nothing."

Gam Gam closed and locked the doors, then clapped her hands, gathering everyone's attention. "All right," she said, grabbing her own lantern from Sloughy. "Off we go to the Church of Savoryn."

Gam Gam led the way into the crowd, Gerald and Sloughy helping to create a much larger bubble than they normally received. Emil tripped a few times, unable to keep his attention on his feet as he stared at Sloughy.

"What are you staring at?" Mina asked.

"His eye," Emil said. "How's it staying in?"

Mina watched the zombie walk, its gait awkward and stilting, its head lolling and rolling around. His one remaining eyeball rolled around like a die in a dice cup but never fell from the socket.

Mina tripped and caught herself.

"I don't know," she admitted, unable to stop watching in case it did fall out.

The Church of Savoryn was a decrepit cathedral on the outskirts of the city, neighboring a retirement community and not much else. It was not particularly tall or grand and there was a large hole in the roof that was not meant to be there, as some holes tend to be. The windows were boarded up, the stained glass long ago removed and sold.

Behind the church, partially boxed in by a rotten fence, sat a small graveyard with twenty-four graves. Gam Gam found a section of decayed fence and slipped through. Emil was unnerved at entering the cemetery. Mina was unnerved at the casualness with which she was getting used to cemeteries. Gerald and Sloughy didn't appear unnerved at all.

"This isn't a very big catacomb," Mina said, glancing around.

"This isn't catacombs at all," Emil added. "Otherwise, why would we need lanterns?"

"They were sealed off long ago," Gam Gam said, walking among the graves and peering at the weather-worn tombstones. She held up the small white paper the soldier had included in the payment. "I was informed of a secret passage that should still be viable here."

Nugget hopped from one gravestone to the next until he stopped on a nondescript one near the edge of the cemetery. Gam Gam looked at the tombstone, then back at a piece of paper. "Oh! Good job, Nugget. You found it."

The cat, who'd curled up on the tombstone, lifted his head lazily just long enough to glare at Gam Gam, then settled down to sleep. Gam Gam stooped in front of the grave and rubbed at the stone, revealing a barely visible violet gem at its center. She tapped it and the gem sank into the stone. The marker then shook and a startled Nugget jumped from the stone and scattered behind Mina and Emil. The headstone slid across the quaking ground and a black abyss appeared where it had been, opening like the jaws of a massive monster ready to swallow them. When the tombstone stopped shaking, Gam Gam glanced into the hole before looking at the others.

"Well, there's a ladder. Now seems as good a time as any to light our lanterns." Emil and Mina stared at her in horror.

Sloughy and Gerald went first, lanterns crooked in their elbows. Nugget returned to his perch on Sloughy's shoulders for the ride down and the zombie did not seem to mind, giving the skeletal cat a soft pet—which left bits of finger in the cracks of Nugget's skull—before grabbing onto the ladder. Gam Gam closed her eyes, sharing Nugget's vision as the undead descended into the catacombs below.

"All clear," Gam Gam said as she opened her eyes and then settled onto the ladder with a grunt. Emil and Mina shared a glance, then Emil shrugged and followed the necromancer down. Mina took up the rear, enjoying the last of the sun before she entered the inky black below.

She had barely cleared her head before the grave closed, causing her to squawk and nearly lose her grip on the ladder.

"Are you all right?" Emil asked in a strained whisper.

Mina clung to the ladder as dirt rained down on her. "Just fine," the nearly decapitated girl said. She took a deep breath once the ground stopped moving and shook what dirt she could from her hair. Her mood improved when she heard Emil choking and coughing at a newfound cloud of dirt falling on him.

Mina stepped from the ladder, ran her hands through her hair, and shook out her clothing, clumps of dirt dropping around her.

"Did the exit close?" Emil asked, looking up the ladder and presumably seeing nothing above.

"Yep," Mina said.

"Is there a way to open it from in here?"

"How should I know?" Mina hissed. "I don't have the paper."

Emil quieted, a nervousness draping around him like a cloak. Mina sighed and put a hand on his shoulder. "I'm sure there's a way back out up this ladder."

Emil nodded, but his confidence did not return. He looked around the small room, a box of four dirt-caked walls with one exit, and shivered. Mina felt it echo within her. This was starting to resemble a grave too much for her tastes.

Gam Gam strode down from the tunnel, two faint lights behind her as the undead moved on. "Everything all right in here?"

"The way out closed," Mina said, pointing to the grave above. "It just worried us a bit, but there's a way to open it from this side, right?"

"Hmm," Gam Gam said, looking up the ladder. "I guess that's why the note suggested leaving someone behind. I just thought it was to stop anyone falling in, but it's probably to help us get back out."

Mina lost all control over her lungs. She had never needed to think about breathing before, it had just happened. But now, *now*, she had to think of it, force her lungs to take in air even as they had no desire for it. When she tried to speak, this lack of lung control led to nothing but a short moan escaping.

But Emil echoed her sentiments exactly. "*We're trapped?*" His eyes were wide with panic, the whites completely visible. His hands shook and his breathing was loud and ragged.

"No worries," Gam Gam said. "There are plenty of entrances and exits to the catacombs and they'll be much easier to find from inside than out." She flashed a smile and Mina felt the trust from it wipe away her doubt. Not all, some fear remained, but Gam Gam's unwavering confidence helped settle her nerves. Her breath returned without needing conscious thought.

Emil was less convinced and even in the dull lantern light, Mina could tell he had turned a shade paler.

"Don't worry. I have a plan," Gam Gam said, a hand on his shoulder. She winked and Emil nodded with a sigh. Then she turned and led the way down the tunnel. Mina ran a finger along the walls here, which were so smooth they almost felt wet. Her finger slid along with ease, not a speck of dirt to be found. When she lifted the lantern to inspect them, the walls were just a flat, dull brown. Nothing to indicate their magnificence.

The tunnel widened at its end, spilling out into a massive chamber. Faint runes glowed along the walls, not enough to see much but enough to tell the size. The entire market square could fit within this space.

The light of their lanterns added closer detail, particularly that, although the market square could fit, most of it would plummet into an inky black abyss. Mina and Emil stepped out to a small pathway that could comfortably fit the two of them and gave the edges a wide berth as they appeared to drop off rather harshly. The path stretched out to the center, where a large circular platform sat with several branching pathways stretching out. Between every path was that same, sudden edge and a drop into nothingness.

"Careful," Emil said, standing at the edge with her. "Looks like it might hurt if you fall."

"I'm not entirely sure there's a bottom," Mina said. If there was, her lantern certainly couldn't find it.

"Well then, it'll be a very boring drop and that sounds worse." Emil stepped back and headed quickly to the central platform. The darkness clung to her as if to pull her down. She quickly followed Emil, not wanting to be on the thin path longer than necessary.

Gam Gam stood at the center, pushing something back into her purse and then clapping her hands together. Her lantern sat on the ground, freeing up her hands as she pulled out the map. A flicker of movement at the edge of the light drew Mina's gaze and she caught sight of the tail of a rather large centipede as it slithered out of sight. She jumped and crashed into Emil who pushed her away grumpily, muttering about jumping at shadows.

Well, something was alive down here. Other than them, of course. She wasn't particularly keen that it was bugs. Mina kept turning, feeling the tendrils of darkness reaching out to her, tugging at her, sliding across her skin. Was it bugs or was there something supernatural here? She didn't particularly—

"Hello!" Emil shouted into the darkness and the darkness replied a dozen times over with the echoes of his own voice.

"Shut up!" Mina hissed, echoes in the darkness agreeing with her. Emil grinned with mischief gleaming in his eyes.

"This is really cool; you never see fancy tombs like this anymore. Who do you think these people were?"

"What if something hears us?" Mina whispered, again feeling the darkness reach for her.

He shrugged. "Gam Gam said there's probably nothing alive down here."

"Except that I just saw something over there." Mina pointed, though she didn't want to say it was a centipede. Then he would mock her for fearing bugs.

"Probably shadows," he mocked anyway.

"You weren't this brave a few moments ago." Mina glared at him, arms crossed, the heat of the lantern warming her side.

Emil shrugged. "Gam Gam said she'd get us out of here. I'm choosing to trust her. What other option is there?"

Gam Gam folded the map and picked up her lantern. "All right, you two, I think I've found the path forward." She pointed down one of the dozen or so pathways with confidence. "Oh, and try to be quiet in case there's anything down here."

Emil's eyes widened and his face paled. Then Gam Gam chuckled and patted him on the head. "I'm kidding, dear. There shouldn't be anything. But if you spot something, tell me. I'll make sure it's nothing dangerous."

Mina stuck her tongue out at Emil and he glared back at her. Then she turned and followed Gam Gam and Sloughy down one of the paths, with Gerald taking the rear. Mina looked out at the tombs and the glowing runes and wondered about the same thing Emil had voiced. Who were these people? Who deserved such elegant and extensive—

"AGH!" Emil shrieked. A clash, glass smashing, and a clatter.

Mina whirled and for a horrifying instant no one was there. Something had gotten Emil and Gerald. Then Emil's continued yelling brought Mina's attention downward, where a dangling Emil flailed above the abyss, a prone Gerald holding him by his ankle. Spilled oil from the broken lantern flared and Mina jumped back. The flames licked at Gerald, though the skeleton seemed unbothered.

Sloughy stepped past Mina, scarf in hand, and patted the flames out as Gerald hauled a white-faced, crying Emil back onto the pathway. He sat on the ground for a long while, breathing fast and wide-eyed with shock. Gam Gam crouched next to him, wrapping a scarf around his shoulders and comforting him. Mina stood awkwardly, looking away.

"Did you slip?" Gam Gam asked kindly, not reproachfully.

Emil rubbed his eyes and took a deep breath. "It was the strangest thing. I was looking down the side of the path and I think it was a roach, it ran right past me. So large it startled me. When I jumped, my foot came down right on the edge and my ankle turned. Then next thing I knew, I was falling down the side. At least until the skeleton grabbed on."

"See," Mina said. "Told you there were living things down here."

"Yeah, but…" Emil chewed on his tongue for a moment before continuing. "This roach had a little piece of yarn wrapped around its neck."

Mina froze, the wheels of her brain spinning. "Yarn?"

"Oh," Gam Gam said, startled. "I'm sorry. I meant to tell you, but it completely slipped my mind." The necromancer held out a finger and there was a faint sound of buzzing as a wasp flew from the darkness and landed on Gam Gam's finger. Mina's instinct was to swat at it, but she wasn't close enough to reach. Emil's was to scoot farther back, luckily staying on the path this time. The wasp stood on the tip of Gam Gam's finger, a small piece of yarn tied around its neck like a scarf. The necromancer smiled. "We have a few friends helping us out today."

"How?" Mina gaped.

"They're all dead," Gam Gam said.

5

"Why do we need the bugs?" Mina asked, stepping around the undulating ground. Gam Gam's hundreds of bugs swarmed the floor of the tunnel as they raced ahead down another snaking pathway. They had walked through three more massive chambers like the first, the necromancer stopping to consult the map each time as the swarm of undead insects ran between their legs, returning from one of the many untaken routes behind and spreading out along the ones ahead. They constantly searched every pathway despite Gam Gam's map leading them right where they needed to go. It seemed a lot of work when Gam Gam didn't seem worried about anything else being down here.

"I second that," Emil said with a groan. Luckily, his ankle was undamaged and he was able to walk along at a normal pace. The loss of the lantern didn't bother him too much either. He had been offered Sloughy's, but Emil had waved it off and just stood closer to Mina. He had mumbled something about liking having his hands free.

"I am using them to scout the tunnels ahead and verify our position," Gam Gam explained. "There's a chance something could be off with the map. This is to ensure we don't get lost."

"Couldn't you have used cats like Nugget?" Emil grumbled.

"Have you ever tried to carry around the bones of this many cats?"

"No," he admitted.

"Where did you even find this many dead bugs?" Mina asked.

"The market sells many strange things. I've been stocking up with each trip." Gam Gam halted down the hallway and stared ahead, though Mina couldn't see anything. "Oh dear," she huffed. Then the tide of the bugs reversed. "Cave-in ahead. We'll have to find a way to circle around."

Gam Gam set the lantern on the ground and pulled the map out, tracing the paths as they figured out a new route. Mina scrunched her feet closer together, trying to avoid the bugs that ran by.

"Do you think there are giant lizards down here?" Emil asked Mina. "Feasting on the bones of the dead?"

"What? Why?"

"Thought I saw something lizard-like back there," Emil said nonchalantly. "Maybe they have a taste for human flesh."

"Shut up!" Mina pushed the boy and he stumbled back, his foot crunching as it landed on the ground.

"Please watch the bugs, dears," Gam Gam said with a knowing look as she packed away the map.

"Oops," Emil said, lifting his foot. A ball beetle with a cracked shell pulled itself forward slowly, its little scarf dangling by a thread. "Sorry," he muttered.

"I think I found us a path," Gam Gam said and they shuffled back down the tunnel after the stream of bugs.

"You didn't really see anything lizard-like, right?" Mina asked.

Emil shrugged. "Who knows? It's pretty dark in here."

"Gam Gam would have told us if she saw anything living."

"Can't imagine she's watching through all those bugs at the same time though."

Mina glared. "If anything is down here, I hope it eats you first."

Emil chuckled and Mina felt a strange lightening of the mood. Yes, they were seemingly trapped down here, winding through maze after maze of tunnels, drowning in darkness. But it also seemed like an adventure again and she was almost having fun.

Mina caught Gam Gam looking back at the two of them, a smile on her lips, before the necromancer turned and led them on through a few more large chambers. As they entered a tunnel, Mina turned to Emil. "There was a rhinoceros down the path back there. But big and scary, with fangs dripping with blood and six horns."

"A rhinoceros? We would have heard that moving," Emil scoffed.

"Who said it walked? It had little tiny wings that held it aloft."

"Tiny wings?" Emil laughed. "How are tiny wings going to hold something that big up?"

Mina shrugged. "Don't know. That's just what I saw."

"Yeah, well, I saw a half-man, half-rat thing down the tunnel I looked into. Slobber dripped from his snout as his teeth chattered. Thin as a skeleton too, so probably starving. Looking for a nice little meal in a young girl perhaps."

"Me?" Mina feigned a shocked surprise. "Despite Gam Gam's best efforts, I'm not nearly large enough to make for a tasty snack. You, on the other hand, did just devour a ton of Gam Gam's cookies. You'll be much sweeter."

"Rats don't like sweet. They like stringy meat and bones."

"That's not true. I definitely saw a rat eating cake once."

For what seemed like hours, Gam Gam and her army of bugs led the way through the tunnels until Mina was sure they were winding around in circles, though the necromancer's confidence never wavered. Twice, she paused halfway down a tunnel and found a crack barely large enough for them to fit through, which led off into another chamber. Each chamber was much like the first: strange glowing runes highlighting dozens of tombs and the endless abyss below. A few times, Mina saw stones like her luxore carved and shaped into elegant designs above the tombs. The glow dulled as they entered with their lanterns and brightened as they left.

The dark continued to encroach on Mina, though a lot of what she was feeling she now recognized as Gam Gam using necromancy. She hoped they found what they needed to sooner rather than later. Despite the teasing and joking between her and Emil, the feeling of being trapped and lost began to sink into her spirit. She was anxious to see the sun, to run around without fear of dropping into an abyss.

The blackness in front of Gam Gam turned solid as the tunnel reached a dead end. Mina pulled up short, a pulse of panic shooting through her limbs. They were always so close, then a cave in or collapse kept rerouting them. Why couldn't they just get there already?

Then Gam Gam reached forward and pushed. The wall swung open like a door. Not just *like* a door, it *was* a door. Mina practiced her breathing, trying to calm herself as they stepped into a hallway. It branched in two directions, but unlike every tunnel they had passed before, this one was lined with doors.

"What is this?" Mina asked.

Emil, curiosity getting the better of him, opened one of the doors and peered into the darkness. "I think this is the poor people's section."

"That does seem to be the case," Gam Gam added.

Mina looked into Emil's room and saw caskets lining the wall of the room and spiraling into the center. Mina shivered.

Gam Gam led the way through labyrinthine twists, down hallways bathed in choking darkness, and through large chambers glowing with luxore.

"We're almost there," she said after a glance at the map. "Should be just down this last hallway."

Emil sighed with relief and pulled open a rusty iron door for Gam Gam, Mina, and a swarm of undead bugs. The hallway stretched endlessly, littered with doors to either side. Hopefully, Gam Gam knew which door, because there were a *lot* of them.

Mina glanced down as the undead swarm dispersed, each bug crawling through the cracks in the door. Gam Gam continued left and the kids followed.

"I believe it's near here," she said, slowing as she glanced to either side. She paused and closed her eyes. "The bugs should be able to help speed things along."

Mina turned to find Emil trying to open one of the doors.

"What are you doing?" she hissed, rushing over.

"Figured I'd see what's in here."

"It could be something dangerous."

"Nothing's dangerous down here, except falling into something." With a final jerk, the door creaked open to a cloud of dust. "Ha! Got it—Agh!"

Where Emil expected flooring, he found none, his body instead pitching forward off balance. Mina grabbed at him and felt the fabric of his shirt slip through her fingers. Her heart stopped as she yelled out.

"Oof," Emil grunted as he hit the ground, which happened to only be a few feet lower than where she stood. Mina raised the lantern and found the room to be a small rectangle, a few feet wide and about seven long, with the ground torn up to create an eerie hole.

Emil thought the same and voiced it so. "I think it's a casket." Then realizing where he was, he jumped up with a groan and climbed back out.

"At least there's no body," Mina said after pulling him out.

"But it looks like there was." He shivered. Then he turned to Gam Gam, who watched with a relieved expression. "No offense, Gam Gam, but I'm not really used to being near corpses yet."

"No offense taken, dear," she said. "Try to be more careful, though. You seem to have a habit of finding pits to fall into."

"It was just two times." Emil glared. "It doesn't happen *all* the time." Gam Gam smiled, but worry creased her brow.

"Is there an issue, Gam Gam?" Mina asked.

"The room should be around here, but I'm not finding it." She looked up and down the hall as beetles crawled back to her. "None of them are reporting seeing the stone. They're all the same sort of small rooms with torn up floors."

Emil wandered over to another door and tugged it open.

"Didn't you learn your lesson?" Mina placed her hands on her hips and raised an eyebrow.

"Just get over here," he said, squinting into the dark room.

Mina reluctantly stepped over and raised her lantern. The room was much the same as the one Emil had climbed out of. Torn floor, barely wider than the door.

Emil ran a hand along the right side of the wall, flush with the door. Then reached for the other wall farther from the door. He ran down the hall to the next door. "Come on!" he shouted as he tugged the door open.

Mina chased and raised the light to an identical room. Emil laughed as he stepped back.

"I think the darkness is affecting you," Mina mumbled.

"No, didn't you see it?" He turned to find Mina staring as if he had grown another head.

"See what?"

Emil rolled his eyes. "Look." He reached inside the room to touch the right wall, an arm's length away from the door frame. Then rushed back to the second room. "This room's right wall is flush with the door." He walked over to the room he fell into and ran a hand along the left wall. "And this room's left wall is flush with the door, but the other rooms' walls butt up against each other."

He stepped back from the room and stood in the spot between the first two rooms. "So what's here?"

"A wall," Mina said.

Gam Gam smiled and placed a hand on Emil's shoulder. "Good find, Emil. Perhaps there is a hidden pathway."

Mina flushed with embarrassment. "A wall with a hidden path. Obviously," she mumbled.

A rush of bugs swarmed the area, then several climbed up the wall. They filled every inch, legs, shells, and wings endlessly shifting as they crawled over each other. Then as suddenly as they'd started, they all ran back down the wall and climbed up Gam Gam's dress and into the large bag propped open within her purse.

"It seems you have made a discovery," she said and stepped forward to press a hand against a piece of stone flush with the wall. It pressed inward and there was a loud clunk that shivered through the ground, then the wall shook and lowered slowly. Between the two rooms, a gap opened to show a narrow tunnel forward. "We found our secret path."

Emil laughed and pumped a fist, but Mina stared down the tunnel, from which a faint white glow emanated.

"Won't we need those on the way out?" Emil asked.

"I left a few to mark the way, they'll help direct us. There should be several exit options I found as well, each marked by my little, many-legged crew."

Before the door slid firmly into the ground, Mina stepped into the tunnel, drawn by the illumination.

"Careful, dear," Gam Gam said, closing her satchel of bugs as Emil hurried after Mina. "Careful, *both* of you." Then she squeezed in behind them.

The tunnel turned and opened into a large chamber in which caskets spiraled toward the center, where a shrine stood. A calming light radiated from within and bathed the room in white.

"Whoa." Mina stared, eyes wide.

"You can say that again." Emil stared down at the floor just in front of them, his own eyes wide.

Mina smiled and stepped forward, excited to race to the object at the center. To the—

"Mina!" Gam Gam shouted. Emil's head jerked up and his hand flashed out to grab her wrist. With a ruthless tug, he pulled her back and into the wall.

"What's wrong with you?" he growled.

"Ow." She jerked her hand back from his grip. "What's wrong with *you*?"

Gam Gam squeezed through the door with a huff while Gerald and Sloughy waited patiently in the hall behind. Then she brushed her dress free of cobwebs and dust. "I thought Emil was the one I had to worry about stepping into the abyss," she noted.

"What?" Mina looked over in confusion, then back where she'd stepped. At the solid ground.

"I don't know if this is the right place," Emil said. "But I'd rather not take the fast way down if it's all the same to you."

He stared at the ground again, as did Gam Gam. Mina glanced between the two of them, confusion growing as the firm ground remained just that.

"What?" she mumbled.

"I agree," Gam Gam said to Emil. "There is a glow down there, but I don't think it's safe to drop down. We could send a beetle to investigate." She began to reach into her pouch of bugs and Mina huffed.

"What are you two talking about?"

They now stared at her in confusion.

"The large pit," Emil said.

"*What* pit?" Mina asked. Gam Gam's eyes widened as Emil still stared at her like she had lost her mind.

"Mina," Gam Gam said, "what do you see?"

"It's a normal room, bunch of caskets. And a glowing shrine at the center."

Now Emil's eyes widened as he looked at Gam Gam, who smiled.

"Is there an illusion, Mina?"

Mina's eyes widened. She had grown so used to seeing past the illusions of Sebastian and Nora, she hadn't considered she could be blocking out other illusions too. With an effort, she focused her eyes and a pit formed in front of her. A red-orange glow from deep within burned upward and all sign of the white glow had disappeared. The edge of the pit began right where she had been about to step, where Emil had pulled her back.

She felt the thrum within her as she pulled on her neuromantic power. Thin tendrils reached forward and she could feel the power of the illusion. How had something like this held for so long? How had it held at all? She'd had no idea illusions could persist after she created them. But this thing seemed to live on its own. How much longer would it survive if left alone? How long had it survived already?

Mina smiled, guessing she wasn't going to get an answer to the former question. Her tendrils stabbed into the room's thin neuromantic coating and she siphoned its power, gasping as it rushed within her. Her stomach churned as if she had eaten too many cookies, but she held on to the power and it soon settled down.

Emil and Gam Gam gasped, though for different reasons. The truth of the room had been revealed to them and now they stared at the glowing shrine.

"Whoa," Emil said, then raced forward.

"Hey," Mina shouted, giving chase. "I got rid of the illusion. I get to see it first!"

"Careful!" Gam Gam shouted, but she smiled as she followed along. "And don't touch anything."

Mina and Emil stopped in front of the shrine and stared at a glowing stone within. It was a bit oblong, though completely smooth, and the light shifted and pulsed as if to a heartbeat. She lifted a hand to grab it, but remembering Gam Gam's warning, she held back.

"What is it?" Emil asked.

"A rock, I think," Mina said.

"I've never seen a rock glow like that."

"Mine glows," Mina said, holding up her ring.

"That's just luxore! Not exactly uncommon." He grabbed Mina's lantern and held it in front of the stone. "Besides, luxore doesn't glow like that and the lantern doesn't affect it."

Mina watched the stone; her gaze was drawn into the depths of the pulsing light. For an instant, she thought it flickered with color, only for the cool white to take over again. Emil said nothing if he saw it.

"What's etched on it?" Emil asked as he leaned closer.

Mina peered too and beyond the light, she could see the soft etching. It was the Tree of Life, just like on a mage's medallion. She gasped, saying so. "Maybe it was made by two elemancers!" she suggested. "A light and a stone one."

"It was actually made by neuromancers," Gam Gam said as she walked up to them. Sloughy and Gerald sidled up to either side of the shrine and stood there. "At least that was the rumor. A hundred of them focusing on a singular object for six days and six nights." She stared at the stone in awe. "I've been looking for this for nearly four years now."

Four years ago would have been while Gam Gam had been at the mage's university, studying necromancy. Only a year after her family had died in the fire. Mina bit her lip, a few puzzle pieces seeming to click for her on what this stone might do.

"What is it, though?" Emil asked.

"It's called the Wishing Stone," Gam Gam explained. "It is said to grant any wish the user asks of it. You just hold it in your hand and ask. Nothing is outside of its power. With this, Mina, you can wish your father back to life and you won't have to worry about the side effects of necromancy. He'd be fully revived."

Mina's heart halted, requiring her own force of will to restart it. Her throat clenched and her mouth dried out. One hand clutched at the rings through her shirt as she bit her lip harder, pushing away the thoughts that crowded her mind. The thoughts that told her to grab it. To make her wish that instant. "Four years," she muttered. "Not five months."

"What's that, dear?" Gam Gam asked.

"Why were you looking for this for four years?" She knew the answer. She didn't have to ask.

Gam Gam's smile slipped and Mina knew she was right. "It doesn't matter, Mina. It's a chance to bring your father back."

"It was for your family, wasn't it?" Mina said, tearing her gaze from the stone and facing Gam Gam. She pushed away the tears that threatened her. "I can't take that away from you, Gam Gam!"

"Mina—"

"No." Mina shook her head defiantly, blinking hard against the welling tears. "You've been searching for this for your family. For your *grandkids*. I can't just steal your wish. You found it, you should use it."

"It's not a one-time thing," Gam Gam said, a forced smile coming back to her lips. Mina saw through it, saw the tears forming in the older woman's eyes too.

"Then you use it first," Mina said. Gam Gam's eyes slid from hers and she knew the necromancer was hiding something else. "It can't be used twice, can it? Otherwise, you wouldn't be so focused on me using it."

Gam Gam smiled, a deep sadness to it. "You're far too perceptive for me to try to hide anything," she said, then sighed. "It can be used multiple times. As far as anyone's aware, anyway." She paused, eyes closed. "Unfortunately, there is a rather large period after a wish in which it can't be used."

"How long?" Mina asked. She felt like she had swallowed one of Gam Gam's bugs.

"As far as anyone can guess, hundreds of years."

A chill ran through Mina. They would only get one wish after all. One wish. Gam Gam's family or Mina's papa. She wrapped her arms around herself and stared at the stone. Her heart ached as she spoke, a dream held in front of her and torn away. "I can't do it, Gam Gam. I can't use it knowing you won't be able to."

Gam Gam's gaze fell and Mina knew she had felt the same. It was why she had tried to trick Mina into using it. Neither of them could forsake the other's family forever.

"Well, if neither of you want it," Emil said, eyes wide as he listened to the exchange. Then his hand shot for the stone.

"Emil!" Mina grabbed at his arm even as he reached out. His hand slammed short of the stone, lightning sparking out from the shrine and knocking everyone to the ground. A storm burst to life within the room, lightning forking all around. Mina's body twitched from the contact, the hairs on her arms lifting but otherwise unharmed. The others seemed the same.

Then strobing blue light filled the room, each brilliant flash leaving a fully armored soldier in its wake. All dressed in gold with the sigil of the Eternal Empire etched onto their chest. Red ribbons hung from their helms. The emperor's personal guard. Swords were drawn in unison, including a tiny knife from Emil. His eyes were wild as he searched for an escape.

Gam Gam struggled to her feet as her gaze searched the new crowd. Horror and sadness pained her face and she turned to Mina with an apology on her lips. The look tore at Mina's heart.

Sloughy and Gerald stepped up beside the group, fists raised. Gam Gam closed her eyes, the air feeling sticky with her magic as she reached out.

"That won't work." A tall man with perfectly coiffed blond hair walked toward them, hand on his still-sheathed sword. His eyes shone hazel in the white glow. "All the bodies have been exhumed from this room and quite a few others nearby. The emperor made sure it was quite thorough."

"Have we broken any laws?" Gam Gam asked, defiant eyes staring down the man. The markings on his chest identified him as a captain. "I have not heard of anything that prevents a few treasure hunters from exploring the catacombs."

"Grave robbing is a crime," he said plainly.

"This is not a grave." Gam Gam pointed at the shrine.

"No," the captain said, then smiled. "That is a trap." He raised his hand and four soldiers with clubs in hand approached. The undead intercepted them but stood little chance, unarmed as they were. Mina shrieked as the two undead were pummeled with clubs and broken apart. Nugget leapt from Sloughy's shoulders, claws digging into the face of one of the attackers. He jumped from soldier to soldier, sharp claws slashing.

Then he was swatted from the air and shattered, his tiny bones raining down onto the ground.

And then they were defenseless and Mina was numb. Tears streamed down her cheeks and Gam Gam stood rigid, face pale and hard.

"Apprehend them," the captain said.

Anger filled Mina and she grasped her power, flooding her veins with it. She would tear their minds apart, every one of them. She would—

Gam Gam's hand fell to her shoulder and Mina saw the barely perceptible shake of her head. The power fled from her and Mina sobbed. The four soldiers who had destroyed Sloughy and Gerald grabbed their arms.

"Wait. Where's the boy?" the captain asked.

Mina's head jerked around and she noticed for the first time that Emil had disappeared. Something seemed to snap within her and she laughed, unable to stop even when a guard yelled at her to do so.

Emil never got caught. He had said so himself and it seemed he'd been correct.

"Forget him. He's unimportant," the captain ordered. He stepped past a chuckling Mina and held a charm up to the shrine. There was a flash, then he grabbed the stone. He stopped in front of Gam Gam, holding it up between finger and thumb. "You've been wasting your time, you know," he said. "This thing doesn't even work."

6

Ominous shadows from the last remaining lantern painted the walls of the empty crypt. The kind of shadows that made one think something moved in the darkness. In this case, it was true. There were two things moving in the darkness.

The first was a boy of fourteen, pushing the lid of a casket loose to slip from his hiding spot now that the stomping sounds of the soldiers had long since disappeared. His eyes were wide, his face pale. He was terrified, forced to choose between being trapped in the catacombs and being captured by soldiers. He was worried he had made the wrong choice. At least if he was captured, he would be alive.

The second was a scuttling of bones slipping across the ground, clacking against caskets and bouncing over cracks in the ground. The sounds grew louder as more bones pulled together.

The boy froze, glancing at the ominous shadows in search of the moving noises. He noticed what they were eventually, which did not make him feel any great sense of safety. At least, not until they began sticking together and took the shape of a small, skeletal cat. Nugget looked up at the boy and mewled. Or he tried to, anyway.

Emil laughed, tears in his eyes, then slapped his hands over his own mouth. He whispered, "Nugget? You scared the hells right out of me."

Nugget stretched. Not that it helped his infernally sore bones, but he remembered a time in which it did. A habit he couldn't really kick. He licked at his paw and scratched at his... well, the space where his ear had once been.

The boy pulled himself free of the casket and brushed away dust and much worse. Nugget felt his minion's presence nearby. No, that wasn't it. She was within. She did that sometimes, looked through him. She could do more than just that. Using her familiar as a focal point widened her arc of necromancy.

Nugget approached Sloughy first. Thick tendrils of necromantic magic seeped from Nugget's eyes, though the boy didn't seem to notice. He prattled on about escaping. At least he quieted when the zombie's limbs reattached and the body sat up. A moment later, Sloughy's head rolled into view and, with a little twist, the zombie reattached his head to his neck. Reformed, the zombie stood and lifted the lantern.

Gerald was easier. A few black tendrils pulled his bones together, much like how Nugget had pulled on his own.

After a few pops and clicks, the skeleton reformed and stood.

Nugget left the crypt, his undead minions following. The living minion chased them with protests. Apparently, he had spoken more, asked questions Nugget ignored. To be fair, Nugget didn't know what the boy expected. He was particularly good at two things and that was ignoring and glaring. He tried the latter when the boy raced in front of him, asking questions in the strange tongue of humans. He understood a few. Gam Gam and Mina were mentioned by name and he pointed down the hallway where they went. Nugget felt Gam Gam's presence in that direction and the boy wanted to give chase. He wanted to fight a hopeless battle.

Sometimes, it was best to regroup, let the enemy sleep, thinking they had won, then strike once more. Nugget had learned that in a previous life. Gam Gam had helped him learn that again in this life when he had faltered. It was a valuable lesson; he hoped the boy would learn it.

Nugget turned around and stretched forward, tail curling high in the air as his rear faced the now speechless boy. Then Nugget plodded on past the boy. The angry boy chased after, continuing with his words, until Nugget halted and sat. It took the boy a moment, but he eventually saw what was right in front of Nugget. That quieted him too. He wondered if the boy understood now or if more bugs would be required before he figured it out.

Nugget didn't wait to find out. He continued, the small beetle racing after him. First, he needed to escape the catacombs, then he would save his minions.

"Gam Gam!" Mina hissed it this time, growing irritated at the elderly woman's lack of response. This time the necromancer heard and she blinked out of whatever daze she had been in. Then she looked down at Mina.

"What is it, dear?" She seemed distracted still, her focus clearly elsewhere. But Mina needed it here, with her. The crowd of soldiers marched them down the hallway and electricity sparked down her nerves with each step. Had the soldiers set a trap for them specifically? Or for anyone? The lack of bodies indicated they'd expected a necromancer. But did they want Gam Gam or did they want *her*?

"What are we going to do?" she whispered frantically. It was a useless gesture; the soldiers were far too close and would hear anything said between them. And though the men were no longer gripping Mina and Gam Gam by the arms, there was nowhere to run with dozens of soldiers filling the hallway before and behind them.

Gam Gam's composure slipped and she placed a hand on Mina's shoulder. Meant to comfort, but Mina could feel the way Gam Gam forced it. "I will protect you, Mina. Whatever it takes."

"But…" Mina mumbled the words, her mind returning to Emil. She was happy he had escaped but worried he'd be trapped down here forever. Was he following them? Was he lost in the darkness? "Emil, he—"

"I'm sure this is all a misunderstanding," Gam Gam interrupted, then ignored Mina's confused glance. "Don't worry about it too much. It helps to focus on some happy memories." Gam Gam smiled, though Mina saw the cracks in it.

"What are you talking about?"

"Like the time we visited your uncle Clyde. Your cousin was there and we all went to the river, panning for nuggets of gold. We even found one." Gam Gam chuckled. "I bet if you asked your uncle, he'd be able to dig up that nugget. It will be nice to see them again."

Mina's breath froze on her lips, her mind racing. The story made no sense, completely fabricated. That meant Gam Gam was trying to secretly tell her something. Clearly about Clyde finding a nugget—no, *the* Nugget. Then her cousin was Emil? Were they fine? But Nugget, he…

"But that piece of gold," she said, breathless. "Last my cousin told me, it was shattered." She looked to Gam Gam, the old necromancer's face warping beneath a sheen of tears she could barely hold back.

Gam Gam's smile was genuine this time. "That was a lie, dear. He was just trying to trick you."

Nugget was fine. Emil would be too. She could have sobbed, but she didn't want to give anything away. Instead, she pushed the tears back and smiled. "You're right, Gam Gam. Focusing on good memories does help a bit. I hope you're also right about the misunderstanding."

Gam Gam's face fell, the truth plain to see. She didn't have much hope about the misunderstanding either. So, who did they want? Gam Gam or Mina?

A shiver ran from Mina's scalp to her toes. A voice inside her head told her she knew the answer to that question. Told her she had dragged Gam Gam into mortal danger again because of who she was. Told her that maybe it would have been better to never have existed at all instead of causing so much harm. She wrapped her arms around herself and couldn't stop the tears this time.

Gam Gam looked ready to console when the captain called out for the group to halt. Two soldiers pulled Gam Gam and Mina to the front and Mina took the time to rub the tears from her eyes. She would not show them to this captain. He would only see her rage.

The crowd of soldiers parted for them quickly, showing the captain and a middle-aged, short woman wearing light armor beneath long gray robes. Strands of gray hid within her otherwise raven black hair. They had stopped at a chalk mark partway down the hall and the woman appeared to be focusing on it or the wall behind it. She pressed a palm just below the mark and the wall melted beneath her touch, creating a large doorway.

She was a mage. A stone elemancer.

She stepped to the side and the captain turned to the soldiers. "We'll be going in small groups, with Raiell ferrying us. First group will be with the prisoners. The rest of you wait here. Raiell will indicate how many can come."

The crowd saluted an understanding and the captain pointed out six soldiers to join them, including the two holding Gam Gam and Mina. The prisoners were shuffled into the room beyond the doorway, a dark box barely large enough to fit the ten of them within. Mina searched for a door but found none. The elemancer must need to open another wall. Instead, she stepped inside and closed the one behind them.

Darkness enveloped them, not a single lantern brought along, and Mina's heart hitched in her chest. Then a soft blue glow formed from her hand. The blue light of the lux-ore filled the strange, enclosed box and Mina remembered Clyde's strong hands giving her the ring. Remembered the man's large smile and easy laugh. A comfort came over her and calmed her.

At least until it felt like her stomach would drop out of her. Mina staggered and Gam Gam put a hand on her. They both looked around at the other soldiers, but no one else appeared affected. At least it seemed Gam Gam was as uncomfortable as Mina felt. She focused on her ring, twisting it on her finger and thinking of Clyde to help to quell her roiling stomach. Whatever was happening, hopefully it would end soon.

It did. The pressure left her and her breathing became easy. Then the wall in front of the elemancer melted. Mina's eyes burned as several torches appeared and filled the small room with light. She squinted, wondering where all the soldiers had retrieved torches from, only to find no soldiers outside. Instead, it was a long hallway with prison cells set into either side.

They were inside a prison now! But how?

"Oh," Gam Gam said, her eyebrows raised. Her eyes sought out Raiell's, though the stone elemancer refused to look in their direction. "That was quite clever. You lifted us through the stone, didn't you? Or was it an already clear shaft and you just lifted our room through it?"

"Quiet!" the captain barked, then directed the soldiers to bring the prisoners before stepping off himself.

As Gam Gam was dragged by, Raiell glanced up and in a barely audible whisper, she said, "There's a shaft." Then she gave a small smile. Gam Gam beamed back and the woman turned red, looking away.

Mina wondered if she felt guilty, helping to bring an old lady and young girl to such a place. Mina hoped she did.

The captain led the retinue down the curving hall, past prisoners who rattled the bars yelling curses and prisoners who curled on the ground moaning and muttering. They didn't bother her as much as the ones who made no noise as they lay motionless in their cells. Lighting was sparse along the hallway, except for a brightly lit side chamber along the inner wall where a portly man sat at a desk. He looked up from a book, thick spectacles enlarging his eyes even more in surprise. He jumped from the desk, book clattering to the floor.

"Captain Delaine!" He saluted. "I didn't expect you."

"Of course not. You had no way of knowing. We need cells for two prisoners."

The jailer opened a large ledger that took up much of the desk and slid his finger down a few pages. "Do they need to be distanced?"

"Unnecessary, but they should be in separate cells." Captain Delaine glanced at Gam Gam, then looked back at the jailer. "Another thing: Make sure to remove all the dead bodies from the area. At least to the other side of the prison."

The jailer paled and looked at Gam Gam, then nodded at Delaine. "Yes, sir."

"My soldiers will remain to assist you, both in protection against the necromancer and to help move the bodies."

"Understood, sir. I have two cells that will work."

"Excellent. I'll be back with the girl later." Captain Delaine grabbed Mina by the shoulders and pulled her toward the stairwell beyond the jailer's desk.

Mina froze with terror, tensing under the firm grip of the captain, her feet locking up and stumbling as he tugged. The captain glared at her, but Mina's world spun around her. Why was she being taken? Why? Why? Why?

"On your feet," he demanded.

Gam Gam stepped forward and three hands grabbed her while every other hand pulled a weapon free. Gam Gam remained standing firm against the threat. "As her guardian, I demand you take me with. I will not leave her unattended."

Captain Delaine stepped up to Gam Gam and glared at her, fire in his eyes. "Funny thing about prison: We don't listen to the prisoners' demands."

"You will regret this, Captain," Gam Gam said. "I will protect that girl, whatever the cost."

"You already failed, old woman." Delaine turned from Gam Gam and grabbed the back of Mina's shirt, pulling her up. "You have the choice of walking or being dragged. The latter will hurt a lot more."

Mina walked.

The world numbed around her. Her body felt nothing, her emotions disappearing into a void, sounds tapering into an inaudible mumble. Whatever Gam Gam yelled after her, she didn't hear. Whatever the captain said slipped through her. She thought she would cry, but she simply felt like a puppet, no thoughts, no feelings, just a hollow wooden cavity controlled by someone else's hand.

Mina drifted through the halls in a daze, a forlorn ghost, listless and lost. It wasn't until she was brought to a stop before two grand, scarlet doors that her mind returned to her, breaking free from the cocoon of emotions. She was in a large, rectangular antechamber with a few chairs to either side.

Captain Delaine ignored the chairs and knocked on the doors. "Captain Delaine escorting the prisoner, sir," he yelled, then dropped to one knee, head bowed. His grip pulled Mina to her own knees, slamming her against the stone floor and sending sparks of pain up her legs. She bit her tongue to prevent crying out.

For a dozen heartbeats nothing happened, though given they were counted with Mina's rapid pulse, this was not actually much time at all. To Mina, it felt like an eternity. Then one door creaked open, agonizingly slowly, and a gaunt man with droopy eyelids peered through and nodded to the captain. Captain Delaine stood, pulling Mina back to her feet, and strode into the room.

The marble floor transformed into elegant carpeting as she stepped across the threshold. Deep scarlets and golds swam across the floor in gorgeous illustrations of the world as it mattered, every bit of land the empire touched. The walls were painted with glorious mosaics of the Eternal Empire's grand conquests. Despite the cleanliness of the room, the scent of dirt hung heavy on the air.

The Eternal Emperor sat on a throne carved of diamond. A gold crown sat atop golden hair. His eyes flashed crimson, the corners rising as he smiled. He barely looked older than Mina; he couldn't have been more than twenty, certainly. She had expected an ancient man, but he seemed young for someone undying.

Mina shivered beneath his inspection, her feet dragging the last few steps, which caused Delaine to stumble. He growled at her and threw her to her knees in front of the emperor. Then he knelt behind her, bowing. "My emperor."

Mina looked away, refusing to meet the emperor's bloody stare, and was surprised to find dozens of people lining the walls of the throne room. Each looked eerily similar with short hair, brown robes, and passive stances. They looked on at the emperor with... It wasn't compassion, but it also wasn't hatred. Duty, perhaps? They looked to him as if he meant everything, not once glancing at Mina or Delaine. But there was something gone from their eyes. Something—

Mina bit her lip to avoid making a noise. One of them was familiar. A young woman, black stubble on her head, brown eyes dull. She wasn't indistinctive, but the loss of hair and the formless robes made it hard to place her. Was she from Mina's village? One of Mikyal's soldiers? Someone else?

"Leave us." The emperor's voice resonated through the room with ease. A man who could command crowds with his natural voice alone. Mina felt it sink into her, felt it force her to look back at him. He still smiled, those eyes sliding uncomfortably past Mina's guard as if drilling into her brain.

Captain Delaine bowed again, then stood and approached the throne, stepping onto a tall dais. He knelt again, hand outstretched, a calm white glow leaking out between his fingers like water. The emperor retrieved the Wishing Stone and inspected it as Delaine rose and left. No one else moved.

"Beautiful, isn't it?" the emperor asked.

Mina ignored it.

"Some tales say a hundred neuromancers, others say a thousand. Some say it took a week to create, others a month. Can you imagine having to use your powers endlessly for a month straight?" He laughed. "It would be rather exhausting. I'm sure you can imagine, yes?"

Mina stared at the floor, holding her breath, begging herself not to give anything away.

"I know you've used your neuromancy at least once to the detriment of one of my worst soldiers. And I doubt you could have retrieved this without disabling that trap." He pocketed the stone and rose from the throne, stepping off the dais directly in front of Mina. "Rise, dear," he commanded.

Mina stood, though she still refused to look up, staring instead at his feet.

The emperor corrected that by grabbing her chin and pulling it up. Not too forcefully, but not gently enough that Mina could deny it.

"Look at me when I speak," he growled, all hints of his smile gone. A chill ran through Mina's body and tears threatened to seep from her eyes. "You *are* a neuromancer, yes?"

Mina didn't respond, frozen beneath those eyes.

The emperor leaned forward and whispered into her ear. The nearness of his voice made it more powerful than if he had yelled. "Answer my questions and answer them honestly or I will kill everyone you care about. Do you understand?"

"You already killed everyone I care about," Mina said, tears falling rapidly. "Your soldier killed my father."

Mina expected a strike or a shout. She expected threats or anger. She expected anything but the laugh she received.

He walked away, shaking a hand at her as he laughed. "No," he said. "No. That was all Mikyal. And that was a *stupid* mistake." The emperor turned back to her, a smile on his face. "A hostage is significantly more useful. He would have succeeded if he had held your father hostage. I know you, Mina. Your father would have been the perfect hostage to get you under control. I also know he isn't the only person you care about. That necromancer downstairs, she's the one who helped you against Mikyal, right?"

"Leave her alone," Mina growled. "She has nothing to do with this."

The emperor shook his head but still laughed. "You misunderstand. I only meant that in Mikyal's situation. I agree with you. She has nothing to do with us." He indicated them both with a wave of his hand and stepped closer to Mina. "I'll probably just kill her." He shrugged.

"No!"

The emperor placed a hand on Mina's shoulder and her voice shriveled away. She ground her teeth as she stared at him.

His smile died on his lips. "Mina," he said. Her name in his mouth felt like an attack on her heart. "Are you a neuromancer?"

Her lips trembled as she tried to answer, but she couldn't. It had been so difficult telling Gam Gam; it was impossible to tell this man. "How…" She croaked the question out, the trailing words falling away from her.

The emperor didn't need them. He smiled. "Did you know when a memory is torn free, it's not removed from the host? It's just disconnected. Nothing a little tampering can't fix."

Mina went pale. Everything she had done to protect her and Gam Gam, it was useless. It was pointless and it had left them vulnerable to the emperor. She felt her knees go weak, almost collapsing beneath her, but somehow, she remained standing. And she continued to stare into the emperor's crimson eyes.

Mina wanted Gam Gam more than anything in the world at that moment. Instead, she wrapped her arms around her shaking body as the world spun around her. "Are you going to kill me?" she whispered.

The emperor laughed. None of Clyde's boisterous guffaw or the soft, warm chuckles of Gam Gam. This laugh sent ice down Mina's spine and her shivering intensified. "No," he said, his smile growing as he ran a finger down the side of her face, brushing a strand of hair back. "What a waste that would be."

"Will you let Gam Gam go?"

"No."

Mina looked the emperor in the eyes even as her own blurred with tears. She drummed up all the courage she could when she spoke. "I won't do anything until she is guaranteed safety."

"You're under the assumption you have a choice." The emperor's voice grew cold and his hand dug into Mina's hair. She yelled and clawed at the hand, her fingernails digging into the skin to no avail. She didn't even leave a scratch. "If you control someone's memories, you control them."

A presence slammed into Mina's mind with the force of a hammer blow to the skull. She yelled out, her knees buckling as she fell to the ground. Two spots of crimson bore through her darkening vision, piercing the cloud and digging into the center of her.

Papa, she yelled. Or did she?

Mina gasped as she woke from a nightmare. Her heart raced, eyes wild as she looked around with desperation. Where was Gam Gam and... and...

"Are you all right, Mina?"

Mina turned. Her father sat in a reclining chair, reading from a book. A cup of coffee held in one hand filled the room with a rich aroma. He had been telling her a story and she had fallen asleep. Everything that had happened, had it been just a dream? Tears welled in her eyes at her relief.

"Papa!" She wiped the moisture from her eyes. "You wouldn't believe the nightmare I had. I met an old lady and you..." Her voice hitched as she remembered. "You died."

"It's okay, Mina. I'm not dead." Papa lowered the book and smiled at her; his crimson eyes seemed to glow. And Mina smiled back beneath their warmth. "Would you like me to continue the story?"

"Yes, please," she said, lying back down on the ground.

"Do you need me to restart?"

"Can you tell me about your first expansion? When you led the Eternal Empire into new lands and conquered them?"

"Yes, dear."

With a deft enough touch, you can erase part of a memory. Mold it how you wish. Alter everything to fit what you want.

Mina wailed into the carpet, her face sodden with tears as her mind crashed back into her body, which shook as she shrieked.

The memory stained her, every flash a coal burning in her skull. She remembered her father in other memories, the kind man he had been. But in one memory, her father was the emperor. Mikyal had killed her father, but the emperor had shown with a single touch he could kill her memories. The last thing she had of him. She grabbed at the pair of rings beneath her shirt and sobbed.

None of the dull-eyed men and women along the walls moved. Of course they wouldn't. Had he done this to them? To Delaine and the jailer? Was there anyone who was not under the emperor's thumb?

"I will teach you to do the same," the emperor said as he walked a circle around her. "I am loath to say this, but I will have need of neuromancers I can trust to control the borders of the empire. That will be your job, to bring the unrest back under control and create a strong, loyal border. I will teach you to act in my name, to become an extension of me. And you will love me for it."

Mina crawled away from the emperor, reaching a hand for the doors, knowing they would not open for her. The emperor stepped in front of her and crouched, peering at her with those bloody eyes.

"It doesn't have to be this painful, Mina."

"Why?" Mina pleaded. "Why are you doing this?"

"I just told you. To—"

"No!" Mina's hands dug into the rich carpet. "Why turn the people against neuromancers? Why have them hunted and killed when you're one yourself? Why keep me alive but no one else?"

"Because you are young," he said. "I can mold you into the perfect tool before you learn what your powers can really do." Neuromantic tendrils crashed into Mina's head, digging their way into her mind.

"Stay out of my head!" she screeched, a sudden burst of her own power pushing the tendrils away, if only for a moment. She pulled her hands over her face and prayed for it all to go away, for her to be anywhere else.

"Such strength. Imagine how strong you can be when you're not cowering behind your emotions. I can save you from that pain, Mina. I can make it disappear."

"Please," Mina whimpered and hated herself for it. "Please, let Gam Gam go. I'll do anything. Please."

A soft hand lifted her chin and the emperor smiled at her. "Don't worry, Mina. It will be all right." His other hand ran through her hair, then paused behind her ear. "The pain will disappear with the memories."

Mina felt the overwhelming presence return, grasping for her mind, ready to steal her memories. And Mina was helpless.

Three rapid knocks rang through the throne room and the pressure stopped. Anger flashed on the emperor's face as he stood and turned to the door. "What?" he roared.

"It's Captain Delaine, sir, with an urgent report," a muffled voice called through the door. A flick of the hand sent an attendant to the doors, which were soon pulled open. The captain stepped in, then knelt, head bowed, but not before he glanced at the prone form shaking on the ground.

"Report," the emperor ordered.

"In front of the prisoner, sir?"

"*Report*," the emperor snarled.

"We have reports of a large army approaching the palace gates," Captain Delaine spoke quickly, eyes wide with fear.

The emperor's eyes widened. "An army? *Within* the city? Who is it?"

"We're not entirely sure, but we have some suspicions based on the report."

"And what suspicions are those?"

"Well, sir, they're undead."

There was a silence that chilled the room and the emperor folded his arms, glaring. "You killed the necromancer's familiar like I commanded, yes?"

"Yes, sir. One of my men clubbed it to pieces."

"Pieces? Were the bones shattered? Did you bring any of the pieces back with you?"

The captain blinked, then tested his mouth a few times before he spoke. "I'm not sure, sir. It broke into several pieces when it was hit. We didn't think to grab any of them."

"Then how do you know it's destroyed?" The emperor's voice was ice.

"It was in pieces, sir," the captain stammered. "We thought—"

"Rise, Captain." The emperor stepped in front of the other man, staring down at him.

"W-what?" Delaine shook as he continued looking down.

"Rise, Delaine."

The captain did as he was ordered, standing in front of the taller emperor, eyes still downcast. The emperor placed a hand on his shoulder and Delaine flinched.

"Your actions have disappointed me, Captain, but there is a simple way to fix this."

Captain Delaine's eyes rose, a flicker of hope shining within. "Anything, sir."

"If you kill the necromancer, the undead will drop."

"Right away, sir!"

"Hold, Captain." The emperor didn't release the other man's shoulder. He smiled, a friendly grin that brought confusion into Delaine's eyes. "How is your daughter doing?"

The captain paused, then blinked as if the question didn't register. "Excuse me, sir?"

"Your daughter, Captain. You have one, don't you? I'm asking how she's doing."

"Yes, sir. I do, sir." Captain Delaine nodded, then smiled. "She's wonderful, sir. We just celebrated her second birthday last month. She—"

The emperor's hand flew from shoulder to mouth as he grabbed the captain's face. Delaine yelled out in surprise, then his eyes went blank. Strange sounds and groans leaked past the emperor's hand as the two men stood otherwise still. The captain twitched, his hands rising as if to claw at the emperor, but too afraid to make contact. Then they dropped to his side.

The emperor's hand returned to the captain's shoulder and he smiled again. "How is your daughter, Captain?"

Captain Delaine blinked, then wiped sweat from his temples and seemed surprised by it. Then he looked at the emperor.

"Excuse me, sir?"

"Your daughter, Captain. You have one, don't you? I'm asking how she's doing."

"Sorry, sir. I don't have a daughter." The man frowned and rubbed at his eye as tears fell. Confusion flickered across his face as he quickly wiped them clear.

"Must have been thinking of someone else," the emperor said as he released the man's shoulder. "You won't fail me again, right, Captain?"

"No, sir." Delaine saluted. "I will kill the necromancer right away."

"Send a crew out to clean up the dead bodies," the emperor said. "And return this one to her cell. Make sure she's there when the necromancer dies." The emperor turned to Mina, crimson eyes holding her gaze. "Tell the jailer to send for me when she's ready for the pain to end."

7

Mina fought. She kicked and scratched, punched and screamed. Captain Delaine dragged her down the halls without breaking his pace. Determination outweighed his morals. Mina bit his hand. *Hard*.

"Agh!" He shook his hand, the motion throwing her to the ground. Mina scrambled away, but not nearly quickly enough to prevent the captain from grabbing her by the front of the shirt and pushing her against the wall. Servants stepped around them without a glance. "Enough!" he growled. "I have no wish to hurt you."

Mina spit in his face, then kicked out. Her shoe smacked the hard metal of his armor and pain lanced up her foot.

Delaine wiped the spit from his face, barely contained anger cracking his facade. "Are you done?" he asked when Mina stopped her flailing and held her hurt foot. It stung, but she didn't think anything was broken. She wiggled her toes to make sure and grimaced.

"How can you serve someone like *him*?"

"He is the emperor."

"And that makes it okay for him to steal your memories? To make you forget your own daughter?"

He hesitated, his anger fading. Then he blinked and pulled her to her feet. "I don't know what you're talking about."

"I won't let you hurt Gam Gam," Mina growled, though each throb of pain from her foot lessened her fight.

Emotion flickered across his face as he whirled at her. His eyes burned with... passion? Anger? Something else? He grabbed her arms and snarled at her. "Listen, kid. You need to learn something here. You are *imprisoned* in the palace of the Eternal Empire. The ruling force of the entire world. No one is coming to save you and there is nothing you can do to save yourself. Your precious Gam Gam will soon be dead. You have no control over *any* of this. *I* have no control over any of this. Bad luck happens sometimes and it's your turn to bear the brunt of it. I'm sorry."

"But—"

"No. There's nothing more to consider. Make your life easier by following orders. Resistance will cause you pain and energy you cannot afford to waste. It is a lesson you will learn quickly. I'll give you time to say your goodbyes and you won't have to watch. Then forget about the necromancer and move on with your life." He pulled her along with a tight grip on her bicep and retraced their path to the dungeons.

Tears welled in Mina's eyes, but they were tears of anger and frustration. Gam Gam would *not* just keel over and die, but Mina didn't know what to do to make sure of that. Frustration boiled within her. She wanted to hit the captain, to tear the palace down around them. She wanted to shove everyone else into their own cells and see how they would like it.

Instead, she followed meekly, pain coming with every other step, fear of that pain keeping her from causing herself more. Afraid and ashamed and frustrated.

He stopped once to send an orderly to the guard's office and relay orders about the undead army. Then she was dragged along the path once again and soon they descended the twirling steps to the dungeons. The jailer jumped from his desk and saluted the captain.

"Any troubles?" Delaine asked.

"No, sir. She's set up in her prison and any dead were moved to a cell at the far end."

"Good. Show me to this one's cell."

"Yes, sir." The jailer led the way and Delaine followed. Prisoners rose to watch, though the rowdiness they had shown at Mina's first visit had died down. She didn't pay them attention and instead focused on the luxore ring, spinning it around her finger. She wondered where Clyde was. Had Emil found him? Were they safe somewhere? She wiped at dampened cheeks as they came to a stop and the jailer pulled out his keyring.

"Mina?"

She whirled toward the croaking voice and found Gam Gam sitting on a bench within her cell. Her face was pale and soaked with sweat, her normally curly hair plastered to her head. Exhaustion seeped from her eyes and Mina felt her own resonating with it. She was so tired.

Gam Gam tried to rise from the bench and stumbled back down. Mina rushed over, grabbing the bars of the necromancer's cell. Delaine let her go as the jailer opened her cell, giving her the goodbye he had promised.

"Are you hurt? Did they do something to you?"

"I'm fine, dear. Just a little tired." Gam Gam smiled and Mina returned it. She hadn't seen the old necromancer this exhausted since Mikyal. She had no doubt who controlled the undead army outside.

Delaine put a hand on Mina's shoulder and firmly pressed. "Say your goodbyes," he said.

Mina looked at him, then back at Gam Gam. "He's going to kill you, Gam Gam!" she shouted and the captain growled and pulled her away from the cells. "I don't know what to do! You have to do something!"

Strong arms picked her up and tossed her into the open cell. Not roughly, but Mina still stumbled to her knees. She turned as the door slammed shut. She grabbed and rattled the door as it locked. "Gam Gam! *Please*!" she cried.

She reached for her neuromancy, but it wasn't there. Not since the emperor. She had been too frightened, her emotions out of control. She couldn't focus, couldn't calm down.

"Is it true?" Gam Gam asked as the captain waved the jailer to her cell.

A flash of something crossed his face, but all that remained was resignation. "I'm sorry, ma'am." The jailer found the key and inserted it. "If there's anything you'd like to say to the girl, now's the time."

Gam Gam looked across the hall to a kneeling and crying Mina and smiled. "I'm sorry, Mina. I love you."

A chill washed over Mina. Her emotional exhaustion hit its end and just failed. She fell into a void where nothing existed except a single spark. She reached for it and neuromancy flooded her veins. In the icy calm, she found it once more. And in that icy calm, she decided she would tear their minds apart until not even the emperor would be able to put them back together.

"If you touch her, I'll strip you of everything you are."

Surprise lit the eyes of both men as they turned to her. Something in her voice and gaze terrified the jailer as the keys slipped from his hand and clanged to the ground. Delaine glanced at the fallen keys and growled as he grabbed them.

"Ignore her," he said.

"Mina," Gam Gam croaked, "it will be all right. Don't worry."

"I won't," Mina whispered.

Mina thrust her power out, hammering at the captain's mind like the emperor had done to her not so long ago. She slammed her presence into his mind and shredded any mental barriers. Delaine stood frozen. Hands shaking, he clutched his head and groaned. But Mina was already where she wanted to be and it was too late to change that.

She stared into the pool at the center of Delaine's mind and reached out. Tendrils of neuromancy fell from her like mist as she spoke.

Everything.

She would strip him of *everything*!

Thousands of memories floated to the water's surface. Hundreds of thousands. Decades of memories of every moment of his life. Images flared within each, butting up against each other for room. A mound formed at the center of the pond as they continued appearing. Mina's tendrils whipped out, ready to haul in the memories, ready to sever them from the man's mind entirely. Ready to—

She froze as one wisp of her magic brushed against a memory and *recoiled*. Her emotions softened, her icy fury turning to a burning curiosity. She felt out the memory like a sore in her mouth and pulled it to her. It was cracked and dull and when she brought her consciousness within, it was like running her brain across a grater.

The memory materialized around her, but it was stilted. The colors wept away like chalk in the rain. People appeared and disappeared, words were spoken in stilted syllables, never running long enough to make sense. The memory died or was in the process of dying.

Neuromancy flowed through the dream, small threads reinforcing everything around her. She wove the fragmented memory together with quick stitches and a pulse of energy filled it with strength once more. It had been so natural, as if she had spent so long knowing how a memory should look, that it made everything wrong blatantly obvious. Like seeing a nearly completed puzzle and knowing what the missing pieces should be.

Figures reformed from a fog she hadn't noticed, now clearing as it took shape. Colors and sounds returned as they should be. A small girl with bright red hair ran, arms and legs flailing as only a toddler's could, and Mina chased her. Happiness and contentment filled her heart. The little girl, her daughter, ran to the arms of a woman. To Mina's wife. No. *Delaine's* wife.

Anger and frustration bled away as Mina watched, felt herself playing with the child, felt the happiness that had been stolen from this man. She smiled as she held the memory in her hand. Vibrancy returned as the face of a small child flashed across it. She placed the memory into the pool and let it float among the others.

She couldn't let herself become like the emperor. She wouldn't toy with the minds of others to get what she wanted. She refused to harm with her powers. But she could heal. She could fix the memories the emperor had broken. She could be more, be *better*. Like Gam Gam.

Images snapped into her mind as her tendrils sought disfigured memories. The gray distortion, color washing away like makeup in the rain. The stilted movement, like puppets with half their strings. She found them and she poured her power within, the neuromancy filling in the cracks and pulling the edges of the memories together. Each contained a young girl with red hair, growing from newborn to toddler. She worked faster and faster as she better understood what she was doing.

Outside her mental domain, time barely seemed to tick by. When she finished, everyone stood in the same location, with only a few changes to their expressions. Gam Gam raised an eyebrow as she looked over at Mina, not the two guards. The jailer stared flabbergasted at Delaine and the captain stared off as tears leaked from his eyes, keys dangling loosely from one hand. Mina drooped against the bars, exhaustion overtaking her.

"Please." Her voice cracked, barely louder than a whisper. "Please, let us go, Captain Delaine."

Delaine's focus returned to him and he stared at Mina. "What have you done?" His voice was quiet, as if he was too afraid to know the truth. His hand shook, the keys jangling.

Then the ceiling exploded.

Rubble rained down as dust cloaked the hallway. Something crashed into the dungeons and Delaine reached for his sword. The jailer cowered where he stood, then screeched as something massive charged.

Captain Delaine had almost pulled his sword by the time an immense, gray trunk slammed into him and the jailer, launching them down the hallway with a sickening crunch. Mina fell away from the cell bars as an elephant stepped past her. It released a deafening hoot in celebration, tusks jabbing into the ceiling and sending more rubble raining down.

Strangely, it also wore a large cloth wrapped around its neck and draped over its shoulders.

"Wanna try that louder, Lyla?" a deep voice growled. "I don't think the emperor heard us." Clyde stepped into view, rubbing dust from his jacket, and next to him stood Gerald and Sloughy and—

"Emil!" Mina crawled back to the bars, a big smile on her face.

"Mina!" He returned the smile, dropping in front of her. "Are you all right?"

"I'm fine," Mina lied. She was going to say more when the elephant began to shrink. Then stand on two legs. Then become a woman. But not just any woman. It was the one Mina remembered from the Dripping Bucket. The one who had been pouring beer on that other fellow.

"Sorry about that," she said with a smirk. "Got lost in the moment."

Emil laughed and Mina realized her mouth was agape. She shut it and stared as the woman tied her long dress at the side to lift the hem. "Pretty wild, right?" he said. "I asked if she could bite me so I could be a were-elephant too, but I guess that's not how it works."

"You would look ridiculous as an elephant." Mina smirked at her friend, studying his face and wondering how it would transform—

"Your sister!" Mina blurted, the words rushing from her. She had recognized the woman in the throne room, but she hadn't been someone she'd met. Just someone she'd *seen*. Someone who was supposed to be dead.

"What about her?" Emil's expression became a mixture of pain and confusion.

"She's *here*," Mina said. "I saw her. In the throne room."

"The throne room?" Emil's eyes grew wide. "Why were you in the throne room?"

"It doesn't matter, Emil!" She shook her head as if to remove the memory of her time there. "I'm talking about your sister. She's alive."

"No, she's not." Emil's eyes darkened, encasing the pain and becoming steel.

"I'm sure it was her, Emil." Mina reached a hand for his, but he pulled away and turned from Mina. "She had shorter hair and plain clothes, but she looks just like in your memory."

"*No*, Mina!" He turned on her and glared, but tears leaked from his eyes. "You don't understand. She might not be dead, but she's not alive. No one comes back from the emperor the same, if they come back at all. They're a husk of what they once were, drained of so much energy they do nothing but lie around and stare at the wall. They don't eat. They don't sleep. They just lie there until they waste away." Emil's fists clenched at his side, knuckles turning white from the pressure. Tears flowed fast from his eyes as he ground his teeth. Then he sighed and wiped his face, looking away from Mina. "Better to think of her as dead."

Mina's throat clenched and she swallowed, hoping to give herself the strength to speak. "But..." Unfortunately, she still didn't have the words. "But she's right there," she finished weakly.

Mina remembered the determined stares, always focused on the emperor. Even when she'd screamed or when others had spoken, their gazes had never flickered. She remembered the smell of dirt and Emil's words played through her head. Over and over. An unthinking husk.

She looked at Captain Delaine, motionless down the hall, though he seemed to be alive based on Clyde and Lyla's conversation.

Then the emperor's words flashed in her mind. She froze at the bars as her mind raced. He had threatened to control her through memories and had proven that it wasn't a veiled threat. He had done it before.

"I can save her," Mina blurted. Emil looked back, his face showing nothing but confusion. Gam Gam sat a little straighter as she listened in.

"What?" Emil asked.

"I mean, there's no guarantee, but I think I can!" She looked back over as Lyla and Clyde finished rummaging through the captain's and the jailer's pockets. "I helped Captain Delaine before you came in. If it's the same, I can help her too." She remembered the dozens of vacant faces. "I can help them all."

"What are you talking about?" Emil asked.

"The emperor. He's a neuromancer like me."

Clyde and Lyla perked up at that, rising from the unconscious guards to look over. Gam Gam rose from her bench and pulled herself to the bars, ghostly white hands gripping them hard. Emil's own expression turned baffled. Sloughy and Gerald simply stared on, unbothered.

"He threatened to change my memories to control me," Mina continued. "I think he really did it with your sister and the others. He modified their memories, so they think whatever they're doing is right. Or is the only thing they can do." She paced her cell. "But I don't understand what he's making them do. They just stare at him all the time. Maybe a personal guard? But then they should be watching for intruders, not staring at him." Mina stopped and shook her head. "It doesn't matter. I'll know more when we find her and I'll do what I can."

Emil turned pale as she spoke and when she finally stopped, he added his own puzzle piece. "She's a vitamancer."

The emperor was collecting vitamancers who focused on healing. Mikyal's memory from so long ago had told her as much. Were they just there to heal him in case of an emergency?

"Sorry to interrupt," Clyde said, "but we have a problem."

"What is it?" Gam Gam asked.

"The keys slid into a nearby cell," Lyla said, looking away from Gam Gam. "We'll have to figure out how to get them before we can get you out."

"No prisoner?"

"Nope," Clyde said.

"Dead body?"

"Unfortunately, no."

Gam Gam sighed. "Well, maybe Gerald or Sloughy can help."

Clyde waved the undead over. "We'll figure something out. Give us a minute."

"I have an idea," Mina whispered to Emil. She dropped to her knees and beckoned him down across from her.

"What is it?" he asked.

"You know how I told you about the pictures I could create for Gam Gam?"

"Sure, you pulled from Gam Gam's memories."

"Well, think of the key." She smiled and Emil mimicked her.

"Oh!"

He closed his eyes and concentrated hard, Mina closing hers in turn. Neuromancy thrummed through her veins, warming her before flowing out in two directions. One to delve into his mind and the other to form his thoughts into reality.

Key.

The memory snapped to the forefront of the pond, a single image of a key floating alone. Perfect for replication. She tethered herself to the memory and channeled it within and into her hands. The neuromantic magic flooded from her fingertips and congealed in her palms. She worked faster than ever thanks to her practice and within a minute, the perfectly smooth, stone-like key sat in her palm. Instead of the raised images she had made before, this one had taken on an exact likeness of Emil's thought. Simple objects she could handle, but it had been exhausting, and she leaned against the bars, content as she handed it over.

"See!" she said. "A key ready to go."

"Whoa." Emil stared at the key, then poked it, surprised when his finger didn't pass through. "This is incredible, Mina!"

He snatched the key, then shoved it into the lock and began wiggling it. And twisting it. And wiggling it some more.

"Um."

"What's wrong?" Mina looked up to see the key was inserted but refused to turn. "Did you put it in the right way?"

"I know how keys work!" Emil paused, pulled the key out, and flipped it. When it refused to enter at all, relief flooded his face. "See! I had it the right way."

"You must be doing something wrong."

"How am I doing something wrong? It's just a lock!"

"Then why isn't it opening?"

"You tell me. You created the key!"

"No, you created the key. I just used your memory of it to bring it into existence."

"Memory of what? I didn't see the jail key!"

"Then what were you thinking of?"

"A key! Any key!" He held it up and Mina looked closely at it and saw the key for what it was. A flat head, with a single shaft from which two comically-long prongs jutted up.

"What are those?!"

"The prongs at the end of a key."

"But keys don't normally have those! They're all jagged at that end. Why would you think of those?"

"Hey, I'm not taking the blame for this. How was I supposed to know the exact key you needed?"

"How different can they be? They're just keys."

"Seriously?" Emil just stared at her, so she glared back. "They're keys! Each one is practically unique."

A loud clatter rang out down the corridor again and the two kids turned toward it.

"Got it," Clyde called. He approached, swinging a ring of keys around a finger. "Good thing these walls are made from pure stone and not mixed. Softened them up and the cell's bars came right out with a bit of help from Lyla."

Lyla pounded after him in the form of a half-human, half-elephant hybrid in a huge dress. A long trunk swung side to side with each step and massive ears lay flat down her back like hair. Her hands were each larger than Mina's head and were shaped more human than elephant, allowing her to easily grasp objects, such as the bars to a cell.

Clyde flipped through the keys and opened Gam Gam's cell. He helped her into the hallway, where Gerald and Sloughy were able to help her stand and walk. Then he came to Mina's cell.

Mina had snatched the memory key from Emil, then tossed it into a dark corner of the cell before anyone could see. Her cheeks set aflame did not help hide her embarrassment though and Emil chuckled until a glare silenced him.

"How are you doing, Mina?" Clyde asked as the door clanged open.

"Fine." Mina stalked out of the cell, arms crossed. Emil looked away and Clyde shrugged.

"We can escape the way we came," Clyde explained as everyone gathered. "I dug a tunnel into the complex that should still be standing. Let's go before someone comes to check on why an elephant is screaming in their cells."

Lyla hooted at Clyde but led the way, glancing around carefully for more guards. Word spread among the other prisoners and a rowdy clamor followed them down the hallway. Each prisoner offered something for their freedom. Most were things that turned Mina's ears scarlet.

Mina stopped when they reached the jailer's alcove, a single lantern burning bright on his desk. The light drew her in and held her firm, even as Emil bumped into her. The others turned at Emil's squawk.

"What is it, Mina?" Clyde asked.

"I can't leave yet."

Only Emil didn't seem confused. "Let's just get out of here, Mina," he insisted, grabbing her arm and tugging.

Mina held Emil's gaze, then turned to Gam Gam. "I don't want to be the kind of person who always runs and abandons those in need. Not when I have the chance to make a difference. I want you all to leave. It's too dangerous to stay here. But I can't. I need to help Emil's sister and anyone else trapped here like her."

"She's not my sister anymore, Mina. She won't be the same. I don't want to lose you too, and for no reason."

"Listen, kid." Clyde stepped forward and crouched to her eye level. "We're lucky to have made it this far and every second we waste, more of our luck drips away. It's only a matter of time until it's gone. We need to get out of here to scheme another day or we'll all end up in these cells and there will be no hope for escape."

"I appreciate all you've done, Clyde." Mina held his one-eyed stare and smiled. "But this is something I must do. Please go on ahead, get Emil and Gam Gam to safety. Even if I'm caught, he doesn't want me dead. I'll be fine."

"You'll be *brainwashed*, Mina!" The fear in Emil's eyes nearly manifested as tears.

"You needn't worry, Emil," Gam Gam said. "Mina can take care of herself and I'll be watching her back."

"Gam Gam…" Mina wanted to say more, but the words choked her. She saw the resolution in Gam Gam's face and knew there was nothing that could change it.

"I will not let you fall into that man's clutches a second time, dear. I'll be by your side."

Clyde stood and ran a hand across his head while Emil pulled away, wrapping his arms around himself and refusing to meet anyone's gaze.

"There was no point in saving you if you're just going to end up imprisoned again!" Clyde growled. "How are you going to search an entire palace without getting caught."

"I have my ways." Gam Gam smirked as Gerald held up her purse. Mina glanced over at the alcove where it must have been tossed before Gam Gam had been brought to her cell.

"I never get caught," Emil said, his voice low. He raised his gaze and didn't flinch away when he found all of them watching him. "I told you that, Mina, and you saw that it was true. So, I'm sticking with you to make sure neither of you get caught either."

"You want to join them, Lyla?" Clyde rubbed his forehead. "Maybe having an elephant stampeding through the halls will be distracting enough they won't even look for you three."

"If it's a distraction that will help," Lyla said, "why not just join the outer battle? Have some fun while we're here. Besides, those zombies won't last long on their own."

Clyde stared at Lyla. "Are you sure that's what you want? There's very little chance we'll escape. Most likely we'll die or be captured."

"At least we go down giving the Eternal Turd a big f—uh, *screw* you."

"Clyde, you can go," Gam Gam insisted. "You have your family to think of."

"You're my family too, Gam Gam." He sighed. "Whatever shady stuff is happening in there, you take care of them and get out of here alive. I need someone to tell my wife that what I did was honorable. Someone needs to tell Shae I did what was right this time."

"Thank you, Clyde." Gam Gam hugged the large man and Mina's gaze dropped. She had consigned these two to getting caught or killed, not to mention what might happen to Gam Gam and Emil. What if it was all for nothing and she cost them all so much? They should have let her go alone. But, of course, Gam Gam wasn't like that. And neither would Mina be like that. "Thank you, Lyla," Gam Gam added as she repeated the embrace with the large elephantine woman.

"Thank you," Mina mumbled.

Clyde pulled her into an embrace and held her tight. "You're a good kid, Mina. You'll be a lot like Gam Gam when you're older and I respect that. Stay safe and remember me whenever your ring shines."

Mina looked up with tears in her eyes and saw Clyde's echoing hers. "I'll do what I can," Mina promised.

"You'll do amazing." Clyde wiped his eye and turned to Lyla, his tone shifting. "Lyla! Let me ride you into battle this time."

"What would your wife think, Clyde?"

"I like to think she'd be impressed."

Lyla rolled her eyes and began to speak when the prisoner closest to them rose from the floor, bloodshot eyes staring out. "You're fighting the emperor?" he croaked.

Lyla and Clyde looked to him and Clyde said, "Looks like that's the plan."

"Let me out and I'll fight with you."

A calm fell over the cells as the words ran down both halls. Then the crude offers from before changed to ones of anger and vengeance. A ringing endorsement for the fall of the emperor.

"How can I say no to such an enchanting offer," Lyla said with a smirk. "Sounds like we might give the emperor a bit more of a fight than he expects."

The prisoner's expression shifted to one of bloody desire. It haunted Mina and sent a chill through her bones.

"Who's ready to fight the emperor?" Lyla shouted and the prisoners yelled back, cups rattling against the cell bars. "Get those keys, Clyde. We have some troops to recruit."

8

Nugget paced the battle lines of his dread army, a ragtag crew of undead armed with sticks and rotten timber, armored with knit scarves, hats, socks, and cowls of a hundred different colors. Some near the back even scrounged up a few bricks or large stones for a fearsome ranged assault. It was an admirable force, which made Nugget annoyed when the humans clearly did not think the same.

They opened the gates and rode out atop grand steeds, wearing furs of metal and bearing sharp sticks made of the same. Not a single face looked worried as they spread out. The undead army still had the numbers, but not by much, maybe only double their adversary. The humans had advantages in protection, durability, and weapons. Nugget would need to make their numbers matter, hit hard and fast. He would not back down from the furless, not while his minion was still held within.

Nugget released a fierce battle cry (which unfortunately was silent due to a lack of vocal cords) and the army responded as waves of necromancy washed over them. They raised their feeble weapons, groaned with their paltry voices, and, as one, pushed forward. Thankfully, there lay a large garden in front of the palace, cultivated into a beautiful creation. It gave Nugget's army the room to maneuver as what flowers could survive winter were crushed beneath dozens of undead feet. Their numbers could tip things in their favor! Invigorated, he rushed with his army, ready to rip the metal furs from the humans.

The furless leader yowled a few orders and they formed a line, pointy sticks dropping to defend their rush. Still, no concern crossed their faces. The horses whinnied and shifted, but they held strong against the stench of decay. He had no choice but to deploy his secret weapon.

Nugget hissed and from hidden locations, dozens of bones were tossed forward, clattering to the cobblestone path before thick webs of necromancy pulled them together. The last to drop were two horse skulls, plopping neatly onto the spines of Sebastian and Nora. The skeletal horses charged straight into the line and the flesh horses bucked, eyes wild. Humans clattered to the ground, either tossed from frightened horses or flung by the undead horses charging into them. Their lines broke and panic flooded as the leader yelled his orders. Shiny sticks swung and prodded wildly and the undead army fell upon the furless.

Organization fled and in its place chaos reigned. The cleanup the humans had expected turned into a full-blown skirmish. Those still upon their horses rode carefully to avoid their friends, which gave the undead ample time to pull them from their steeds. The riderless horses panicked and galloped across the garden, away from man and zombie. The humans turned to their swords as combat closed in, great swings cleaving bones from their attackers. The undead clattered to the ground as necromancy fled their crippled bodies.

Nugget scampered through the mob, ducking between stomping feet to scale the back of a zombie. He leapt from the undead's shoulder to take an attacking man by surprise, clinging to his face with sharp claws and cleaving great ditches into his cheeks. Nugget had hoped to take an eye—he particularly liked taking eyes—but missed. He hit the ground and scrambled away before the furless could retaliate. In his distraction, the human took a brick to the face and dropped to the ground with great amounts of blood squirting from his mouth and nose.

Nugget weaved, searching the crowd for the most troublesome furless and striking quickly. Many pulled down face guards, made aware of Nugget's tactics, to avoid a similar fate to his first victim. Others were too swift and easily ducked around Nugget's lunges. His advantage was lost and his claws were useless against the metal fur. Within moments, the battle turned and their numbers no longer mattered. Efficient swings of their swords culled the undead and opened more space for maneuverability.

They fought in circles, protecting each other's backs and giving no opportunity for the undead to lay a hit. A zombie would dive in, hoping to disrupt their defense, only to be knocked aside by a blade. They hit a standstill, the undead unable to move forward, and the humans took their chance. Pressing forward, herding the army together, preparing for slaughter. Nugget smelled the winds of failure and shame filled him. He had not lost a battle so soundly since he'd last lost his life. He detested it, but no solution presented itself.

At least not until Sebastian and Nora returned. The skeletal horses herded the living ones and chased them into the crowd. Metal and bone scattered as the stampede hit. Nugget darted between legs and jumped onto the face of a downed human, scratching at his metal face to no avail. The soldier reached for Nugget, but he was gone, retreating and searching out a new target. Something he could sink his claws into.

A blade nearly bisected Nugget as it slammed into the ground. He jumped away from another swing and turned to find a man with a shield. Several men. Six surrounded Nugget, four trapping him as the other two swung down, trying to hit him. Nugget's hackles rose as he hissed. He pressured the undead army to help, but the nearest had been felled and the farthest had no clear path. He would have to fight alone. Nugget's claws twitched for blood. He would not be the only one to fall today.

He lunged.

Another blade arced down and Nugget pivoted around it, jumping onto the man's arm. He darted to the side as a second man took a swing, slamming it into the arm of the first. One of the shield men dove and Nugget leapt. He bounded from the shield and dove for the opening created by the clash. He would retreat and circle back, these foolish men would never stop—

A web of rope dropped from the heavens and Nugget's feet tangled with the holes. The skeletal cat dropped and twisted, the ropes catching in ribs and other exposed bones. A satisfied furless grabbed one end of the net and lifted it. Nugget came with it, helpless against the restraints.

"We got the cat!"

"Destroy it!" yelled the leader. "Destroy the necromancer's conduit and the rest will drop!"

The furless tossed his captive to the ground and pulled a small club from his side. Nugget mewled uselessly as he flailed in the netting. It was shameful to be destroyed by as crude a fighter as the human. As if fighting with something other than your own natural skills and abilities was dignified. It was pathetic.

A great roar saved Nugget from such a shameful death as dirt and stone showered the fighters. The man with the club tumbled away even as Nugget was tossed by the explosion as well. A dust cloud flowed over the garden with several figures standing at its center.

Clyde strode into the battlefield wielding fists of stone, a large gray creature next to him with a massive stone hammer. Dozens of emaciated humans gripped their own weapons of stone and spread out. A calm washed over the battlefield as every side evaluated this disruption.

Then Clyde shouted, "Fight like you just escaped prison and don't want to return!" They roared as one, rushing against the metal men with their stone weapons.

Metal crunched as Clyde slammed his fists into the humans nearest Nugget, sending them crashing away. The soldiers recovered from their shock to attack the new assailant, but Clyde deflected one sword blow and slammed a fist into the man's knee, sending him crying to the ground. Then he blocked a second blow and stomped the ground. A great stone pillar jutted from the earth, smacking the soldier in the gut and sending him flying. Clyde dismantled the metal men in moments, sweat shining on his body. The gauntlets melted from his fists like water and he wiped his forehead with newly bare hands, flashing Nugget a smile in the process.

"I've seen worse places to lounge but can't say I'd choose the same."

Nugget hissed, though it did not have the intended effect. Clyde crouched and deftly untangled the net. Nugget bolted from the horrific bindings and shook free that terrible feeling of containment. He nodded graciously to the human elemancer and readied himself for battle once more.

The latest additions had vastly turned the tide of battle. The unsuspecting soldiers retreated into the castle, unprepared for any sort of real battle.

Bells rang from within the compound and beyond the open gates, soldiers flooded the courtyard. Several orders to close the gates sounded out and soldiers yelled to their companions to hurry within.

"If those gates close, our distraction is dead," Clyde muttered. He punched the ground with both fists and the stone reshaped into gauntlets. "To the gates! Don't let them close!"

Skirmishes forgotten, everyone rushed to the gates. Soldiers ran for safety, undead chased at a lumber, and Clyde and his gang ran with fierce determination. Nugget bounded between them, not ready for his battle to end.

A trumpeting filled the gardens and the gray creature grew into a great, four-legged beast with a swinging trunk and tusks. It stampeded toward the gates and the humans' shouts intensified. The doors slammed shut on fleeing soldiers in great panic. Caught between a locked gate and a charging monster, they dove to the side as the gray beast slammed into the doors. Wood cracked and the doors burst open. Guards flew backward and the tolling bells grew wilder. The undead, Clyde, and his gang stormed the courtyard, stomping on the fallen soldiers.

The battle started anew as the Eternal Palace's guard flooded the courtyard. An endless stream of men in metal.

Nugget's heart would have sunk if he had one; there was no way to win this battle. He had to hope that it was enough to give Gam Gam the distraction she needed.

"It's clear," Gam Gam said.

Emil scouted forward, the soft chatter of dozens of legs leading the way down the hall and following them behind. Eyes everywhere, Gam Gam constantly flitted through them to monitor their surroundings. So far, they had not been caught off guard, but Gam Gam was pale and leaned heavily on Mina as they followed along.

"Are you all right?" Mina asked.

Gam Gam's blank stare disappeared just long enough for her to look over and smile. "I'm okay, dear. I understand my limits and we haven't reached them. I'm just a bit stretched thin is all."

Stretched thin was one way of putting it. Mina could hear the rattle of the undead army echoing through the palace halls. What few glimpses she caught out the windows showed a dire scene. They now fought within the courtyard, surrounded by hundreds of guards, and though the guards were being cautious, it would only be a matter of time. If it had only been Gam Gam's undead army... but Mina had caught sight of Lyla and that meant Clyde as well.

Emil waved them into an empty closet and Mina set the necromancer down on an upturned crate. Both let out a sigh of relief.

"Are we close?" Emil asked.

Mina nodded. It had taken some time, but she now recognized the hallway. If they continued, they'd find the throne room soon enough. Either Emil's sister was there or she'd likely be close. This was as good a spot as any to hide as Gam Gam's scouts did their work.

"How is the army holding up?" Mina asked.

Gam Gam took a steadying breath before speaking. "I don't think we have long. We'll have to move quickly."

Moving quickly wasn't something they were doing well, not with Gam Gam's exhaustion. She bit her lip, resolve solidifying within her chest. "Find us Emil's sister," she said, "then work on getting Clyde and Lyla to safety, as well as yourself. Emil and I can continue alone."

Emil nodded. "Once we know where to go, I can get us in and out easily."

"No," Gam Gam said. "I told you, Mina, I'm not letting you fall into the emperor's hands, not without doing everything in my power to stop it."

"But—"

"That's enough, dear," Gam Gam said sternly. "I've made up my mind, as you've made up yours to save this young lady. We will handle whatever comes up. Now, if you could let me focus, I'll begin searching."

Mina paced and worried her lip. Each passing moment chipped away at their chance of escape and increased the chances of her friends facing terrible fates because of her decision. If only there was some way to speed things along.

"I've reached the throne room, though I don't think I see her," Gam Gam said, her brow furrowing in concentration.

"She was just there. Are you sure? Do you remember how I described her?"

"Yes, dear. Though 'Emil with no hair, taller, and a woman' isn't really the best description."

Mina rubbed her eyes. "If I could project the image into your head, then you'd know immediately. But I don't know how to do that." She threw her hands up in frustration. If only she could do what the emperor had done to her, modify Gam Gam's memories so she'd know—

No! Mina shook her head. She would not be like the emperor, no matter what.

"Hmm," Gam Gam pondered, eyes closed. "But you can still see my memories."

"How's that going to help you find out what she looks like?" Mina asked.

"It's not." Gam Gam smiled. "But I remember the faces I saw in the throne room. Scan my memory of that and I'll continue looking through the other bugs. I'll tie all the memories together by focusing on scouting."

Mina's eyes widened. "Right!" She dropped to her knees in front of the necromancer and placed a hand to either temple. Then she tethered to the comfortably warm and familiar mind of Gam Gam.

Scouting.

Only two memories floated up, but one in particular flashed the familiarity of the throne room. Mina shivered but reached out and pulled the memory in, then projected it around her, painting the walls of the closet with the bug's view of the throne room.

Emil shifted uncomfortably, but his eyes were glued to every face that passed through the bug's vision. Mina held the memory for a moment longer where Emil's sister should be. Instead, a dark-skinned male stood in the same clothing, head shaved just as hers had been. And for a moment, Mina doubted herself, wondered if she had made it all up about Emil's sister. What if she had put everyone in danger because of a hallucination?

Another voice asked her if she could trust her memory. How much had the emperor changed? Was this all a trap, and if so, why go to such trouble when she had already been caught?

Then she watched a servant walk in and swap places with another. The other left, dark spots beneath her eyes, a slump to her shoulders. Emil's sister had been replaced too, surely. Mina couldn't let herself believe her memories were corrupt. Emil's sister must be here.

She pulled free of the one memory and moved on to the next. A beetle followed the retreating servant down the hallway and around a bend. Dozens of doors lined the hallway and he entered one. In a new memory, Mina saw within the doors. Small dorms, a single cot and a chest with clothing and nothing else. Several were empty, but many more were occupied by an individual sleeping. If they weren't sleeping, then they lay awake, staring at the ceiling, unmoving. What was going on?

"Mina!" Emil grabbed her arm and pulled her concentration away. The tether snapped and Mina's eyes shot open. But she had seen it too. They had found Emil's sister.

Emil practically pulled them down the halls, Gam Gam's insects leading them down a winding path with no guards. It took both an eternity and no time at all before the door loomed before them. Emil stared, eyes wide, breaths fast, so Mina took the door in hand and inched it open.

There, lying in bed, eyes closed, Emil's sister slept.

"Izra!" Emil slid to his knees beside the bed and grabbed at the hand that rested atop the covers. Her eyes opened and her head tilted. She stared back at Emil without recognition, without understanding. The light in her eyes had died; she was a construct no different than a zombie Gam Gam might raise. "Izra?" Emil whispered.

But she did not respond.

Mina knelt beside Emil and a chill washed through her seeing the woman so close. She placed a hand on Izra's forehead and the other woman did not react.

"Can you fix her?" Emil asked, voice choking.

"I can try," Mina said. Then she did.

Neuromancy hummed through her veins as she tethered to Izra's mind. The great pond materialized before her and Mina poured her power out, asking for one thing: all her memories.

Everything.

Memories popped to the surface. Not in an explosion like they had for Captain Delaine, nor even the swift arrival of most searches she had done before. No, these memories wafted to the surface as if forced through some restraint, rotten and festering. The count so minimal, she could have looked through them all in an instant. She didn't need to, though, as she saw the emperor's face in every one.

This couldn't be all of Izra's memories! What had happened to the others? Her non-corrupt memories, the times before the palace? *Emil?* They were all gone.

The false memories dipped below the pond, not even holding the buoyancy of true memories. Mina called again to the pond, trying to surface every memory, and again she watched the festering wounds of the emperor sink below the waters.

She crouched at the edge of the pond, peering beyond. Always before it had been radiant, light blooming up from beneath, but now it seemed an endless depth. How deep did it go? How deep had her memories been shoved?

A talented neuromancer knows what to look for. The emperor's baritone voice rang through Mina's head.

She needed to know more, needed to understand how her powers worked. She needed to find out. Mina tipped forward and plunged into the depths of Izra's mind.

9

The last of the undead slipped from Nugget's grasp as the furless hacked it to pieces, its bones crumbling to a fine dust. The aged undead from the catacombs had proven mostly fragile. Hundreds of humans in their metal coats surrounded what remained of the living. Clyde fought with a small group of other elemancers, one lightning, one air, and a second stone elemancer. The gray beast, in some hybrid humanoid form, fought with those without magic, protecting them with her thick hide and wide reach.

None of that mattered. The emperor's troops contained mages of their own, easily deflecting whatever Clyde and the others tossed their way. They were surrounded and outnumbered. The battle had reached its conclusion. A resounding loss. It would have raised Nugget's hackles if he had any.

Gam Gam's tug became more insistent, drawing his eyes to the balcony where the emperor stared down at the battle. He would need to leave; he couldn't risk his destruction out here. Retreat was despicable, especially at the cost of everyone else, but it was the only option now. There was more at play than a single battle. His minion needed to escape so he could have his vengeance.

Nugget readied himself. He would need all his quickness to break through the thick crowd. He propelled himself forward, non-existent muscles tense for any sudden turns. He hadn't made it out of the center before a wall of stone materialized from the ground in front of him. Nugget screeched to a halt and glared at Clyde.

The one-eyed man only glanced back. "You're not making it if you run," he said. "They have nets at the ready, not to mention dozens of mages and hundreds of people. You're as good as dead"—Clyde glanced back before amending—"dead *again* if you leave."

The human didn't understand. Nugget would be destroyed if he didn't leave. At least this gave him a shot. He circled around and shot for the crowd again. Clyde raised another wall with a quick step of his foot and Nugget halted.

"I didn't say you couldn't go." Clyde smiled down at the skeletal cat. "Where do you need to go?"

Nugget stared at the palace. The pull was the strongest toward the emperor, but that was not where he needed to be. Impulses directed him toward a different location. He needed to get to Sloughy and Gerald, who were patiently waiting in the dungeon. The first-floor entrances were guarded, however. That meant an alternate route.

A woman stood on the second-floor balcony, watching the battle with awe and worry. The door behind her stood open. Nugget clicked his teeth and pawed the ground. Clyde's gaze followed and he nodded.

"Lyla!"

"Not now, Clyde!" The gray beast roared as she flung the limp body of a soldier into the slowly approaching crowd. Her movements lagged; her strength waned.

"Package delivery, second floor balcony with the onlooker. Below the Eternal Dirtbag." Clyde swung away from the mages he'd faced and turned to Lyla's opponents. He slammed stone fists to the ground and the stone beneath the soldiers' feet melted. The metal men sank and flailed before a stone elemancer could stop his attack. It left the other elemancers open and the emperor's mages pushed forward with a barrage.

"Nugget!"

Nugget ran. He leapt onto Clyde's back and again off his shoulder. Lyla's massive paw grabbed him and she spun him in a tight circle.

"Hold on to all your bones!" She hooted as she launched Nugget through the air. He flew toward the emperor, who looked surprised at the attack, and for a moment Nugget thought the two would collide. Then gravity pulled on the skeletal cat and he fell instead to the balcony below. The woman screamed and fell back as Nugget slammed to the ground, his bones crashing apart in every direction.

She screamed more when the bones rolled back together and Nugget popped back into form. Moments like this made Nugget happy for the malleable skeletal form that had replaced his flesh body. Fully reformed, Nugget glanced back to see the crowd descend upon Clyde, Lyla, and the prisoners. Then he ran into the palace and to his minion.

"We suffered only one death, sir," a man reported to the emperor. Gam Gam watched from the eyes of a beetle nestled in the corner. The emperor strode in from the balcony where he had watched the overwhelming victory of his guards. "The escaped prisoners have been captured or killed, and the two instigators—a stone elemancer and a were-elephant—were captured as well."

"The old woman and the young girl?"

"Not among those outside. We're not sure if they're still in the cells or not."

The emperor looked around the room with cold eyes. "They're not. Her cat escaped into the palace, yes?"

"Yes, a soldier's wife was here and reported the skeletal cat reforming and entering the palace."

"Induce comas for all prisoners. I want no more attempted escapes. Then send the troops sweeping through the palace to find anyone else."

"Wouldn't they have escaped, sir?"

"Why would her cat enter the palace if she had escaped? No, the necromancer is within our walls. When I find her, I will kill her."

"Yes, sir!"

"And one more thing: Have whoever killed one of our men hanged."

"Um, sir, the casualty occurred because of, um, friendly fire."

The emperor glared at the soldier and Gam Gam felt the fear radiate off him from several rooms away. "Did you not understand my order?"

"No, sir! I'll get on it right away!" The soldier scampered from the room.

The emperor stood still, a cold fury seething beneath his skin. His eyes scanned the room, but whatever he searched for was well hidden. "Are you listening, necromancer?" he asked.

Gam Gam jumped. Was it dumb luck? A guess? Or had he found her out?

"You must have some way of sneaking around the palace undetected. Is it bugs? My jailer reported a bag of dead bugs on your person." His eyes scanned the room higher.

Gam Gam held the beetle steady. Movement would only draw the emperor's eyes.

"I will find you, necromancer." His eyes paused as they found the beetle and Gam Gam made eye contact with the

Eternal Emperor. "You will die, old woman, but not before you betray yourself and deliver me the girl. It will be your last act. You can do it freely or I can make you do it."

The beetle fell from the wall and clattered to the floor, inert.

Mina floated in an endless abyss and wondered if she had somehow pulled her mind free from her own body entirely. Maybe she floated in a wasteland where memories went to die. The sudden light blinded and disoriented her, then was gone. The echoes of a question rang through the void.

What should we do?

She was ready the second time and when the darkness broke away, Mina saw what surrounded her. A tree, hundreds of times larger than her perception but dripping with rot. Roots dug deep into the darkness, pulling from somewhere beyond Mina's reach and forming into a massive trunk. Great branches reached out and split like millions of claws grasping for her. Thousands and thousands of gray petals clung to the deadened branches. The strange light pulsed from root to tip of a single branch. One petal flared alive for a few seconds, then everything fell into the darkness once more. The hint of a question lingered in the air.

What should we do?

Mina reached out for where she had last seen a gray petal and touched it. An emptiness hung in its spot, a pocket of absence, a dead memory. She poured her neuromancy within and it flared to life. Mina pushed her consciousness within and watched the memory come to life.

She walked, hand in hand, with a boy. Happiness filled her and her heart thrummed to its tune.

The world melted away first, then the boy. Then there was nothing once more and it returned to the gray color. There were no cracks in the memory, no damage for Mina's power to mend. It was nothing like Delaine's memories. How could she fix something that had nothing wrong with it?

The lights flared again and once more a question sang out. But not the one she had expected.

Did she just smile?

A different branch lit up. A different memory triggered. What had changed? Had she unintentionally activated the memory for Izra as well? Mina reached once more for the memory. Maybe if she gave it enough energy, it could reactivate completely.

Pain lanced through Mina's mind, a migraine trying to crack her skull open. The tether nearly snapped and it was all she could do to hold it together. She wanted to scream, and maybe she did. It was hard to tell.

The light flared and Mina saw it. A black sludge attached to her. She saw her presence being consumed by it and her mind reeled. Still, she clung. She couldn't leave. She had to remove the rot from herself.

Mina?

Mina spun, but the question hovered within the darkness, no source in sight. She bit her lip, or at least incorporeally mimicked the behavior, and focused on what was in front of her. Whatever attacked her wasn't physical; it was manifested within Izra's mind. And the mind was where she was the master.

Neuromancy channeled from within her spirit form and she built it within until it hummed and she glowed a soft blue. Then she pushed it out in all directions, a quick healing burst like she had used on Delaine's memories. The black sludge evaporated from her; she reformed and the pain disappeared. It had worked.

When the lights came again, she saw what else had happened. Not only had she cleansed the sludge from herself, but the branches around her were clear as well. The lifeless memories colored just a bit, but still no light reached up to the branches. Black sludge farther down its base had insured that.

Are you all right?

Somehow, the emperor had to be responsible. He must have coated the branches in the strange mucus to prevent thoughts from reaching these memories. If these memories were hidden, which were left intact?

The answer curdled her stomach. The next time light sprang through, this time without an accompanying question, Mina traced it to the activated memory. The pulse of orange light filled the memory, but it turned a sickly red orange as it triggered. Mina pulled herself within.

Mina was a perfect servant, a gift to the great master. The world was his to run and run it he did. But aches and pains bothered him and it was her pleasure to soothe him always. To erase a world of hurt so that the great master could heal the world. She loved him and he loved her. He was her duty, always and singularly. Vitamancy flowed from Mina and filled the great master, and he turned and smiled. Pride flooded her heart, pride in a job well done. Others soothed the great master and his aches around her, for he had many aches. But she would make sure to soothe him the best. It was what he deserved.

Mina fell from the memory, gasping and nauseous. If she had been within her own body, she was sure she would have vomited. But as a disembodied presence, she had to settle for dry heaving. The memory was wrong, corrupt. She felt the emperor's presence bearing down on her from every direction. It had been fabricated from his very essence. The sky was a canvas, ever-ready for a true picture. The floor was plain and flat, the walls devoid of anything more than the brick that constructed it. The other vitamancers were faceless dolls, dressed identically but ambiguous in features. A lingering sense of loyalty and devotion clung to her and disgusted her further. She wanted to rip the memory free and destroy it, but Mina had to be careful not to destroy Izra's mind in the process. She couldn't risk more damage than the emperor had already inflicted.

But the emperor had given her a way to block off the ruined memories. She only needed to figure out how it worked. She could manifest her neuromancy physically; could a similar process be undertaken here? She'd always had a memory to draw from, a blueprint for her power to follow. This would be unguided. Still, she pulled on her neuromancy and pooled it within her manifested palms. The blue energy formed into a ball and when Mina stopped, it dissipated into nothing.

The sludge attacked her, ate at her mind and at Izra's. But the emperor wouldn't have wanted to battle his own technique every time he entered a mind, and though the goo ran along much of the branches, it never touched his fabricated memories. As the light returned, Mina even noticed a thin trail for the light to run along the branches, as if the emperor had marked it safe from the sludge. So, a defensive structure? Something that attacked everything that wasn't his own mind and thoughts?

Protection, but placed in a mind that was not his, so it acted like a parasite. Leaching Izra's memories away except for the ones the emperor asked for. Izra was a prisoner within her mind, completely unaware. It disgusted Mina and broke her heart.

When she pulled on her neuromancy once more, it was with a different conviction, not one to copy an evil act like the emperor's but one built on love and protection. Mina wanted to mask the rotten memories and heal this woman's mind. The magic pooled in her hands, solidifying into a soft gel. She coated the memory and released her hold. The gel didn't disappear and when the light returned, the memory failed to react.

Mina burst into laughter. She had done it. She had actually done it! She could figure out how to undo the emperor's taint. *A talented neuromancer knows what to look for.* "I've figured it out," Mina growled. "And I'm going to take away all your minions. I will never let you hold another mind under your sway like this."

Mina pulled neuromancy within her until she glowed like the sun, until the pressure grew so intense she thought she would explode. Mina held it until she couldn't anymore. Then it burst from her, a wave of nurturing light washing over Izra's mind. The emperor's black sludge burned away beneath its touch. Mina groaned as she pushed it out with all her power, scrubbing away every bit.

The power faded and Mina spread her presence over the mind, searching for the emperor's touch. Everywhere she found it, she scoured it away or coated it in her own protection. Everything done at the speed of thought, she had already finished when the mind came alive once more. Brilliant colors flared to life, pulsing and filling the tree from root to branch. Memories glowed bright like the petals on some spectral flower. It was like watching a gem shining in brilliant light. Mina was struck by how the mind was the Tree of Life carved into every mage's medallion. Perhaps she saw the tree's origins here. She couldn't imagine anyone seeing this sight and not having it embedded within their soul for eternity. She could have stared at it for hours. But she didn't have hours and she had others to save as well.

Mina slid through the tether and collapsed as physical weariness struck her. Sweat soaked through her clothing as her legs and arms shook. Gam Gam was there, holding her and speaking, but her words fell silent as Emil's grew louder.

Izra's eyes darted around the room as she hyperventilated. They slid across Gam Gam and Mina, then halted on her brother. "Emil?"

"Izra!"

She sobbed as she clung to her brother and Emil shared a few tears of his own. Mina smiled; her promise was kept.

Gam Gam held Mina and proudly smiled at her. "Good job, sweetie," she whispered.

"Are you all right?" Emil asked his sister as they both wiped their tears away. Smiles clung to their faces, unwilling to relent.

"I think so," she croaked. "My head hurts, but I'm so happy that it does. For years, it has felt" —she coughed as she tried to track down the right word— "unused." Then Izra's hand was on Mina's, pulling her into the conversation. "It was you, wasn't it? You were in my head, freeing me from the emperor's control. There's a familiarity to you, as if I should know you."

Mina nodded. "I'm Mina. I'm here to save you and the others."

Izra's face scrunched up as more tears ran down her cheeks. "Thank you," she whispered.

"I'm happy I was able to figure something out." Mina wiped her own joyful tears away before they overwhelmed her. She had more work to do and couldn't let her emotions take over yet.

"Are you able to walk, dear?" Gam Gam asked Izra. "We'll make sure to get you somewhere safe."

Izra nodded as Emil helped her to a sitting position. Physically, she seemed fine, if a bit exhausted. But her head hung low and her hands clung to it as if her old memories overwhelmed her.

"Izra?" Mina asked. "If it's not too much trouble, can I ask you something?"

"I owe you my life, Mina." Izra smiled at her. "You can ask me anything you want."

"Why does the emperor need so many vitamancers to soothe a few aches and pains?" One vitamancer could have done so with ease, but the more Mina thought about it, the surer she was that everyone in that throne room had been a vitamancer. The smell of dirt had been a strong sign of it. Not to mention the memory indicated others of her powers. "Was he afraid of assassination?"

Izra's eyes darkened and she winced as if the memory pained her. "I think that played a small part." She closed her eyes as if focusing, trying to find the right memory in a sea of fresh ones. "But he's... he's so old." A sharp intake of breath and her eyes slowly opened, though they were unfocused.

"Isn't that why he's called the *Eternal* Emperor?" Emil asked. "Because he's immortal?"

"He's not," Izra said, her eyes shifting wildly as though sorting through her information. Then she groaned as she grabbed her head "Not technically. He just makes it seem so. I'm sorry. It's hard to focus. I'm remembering every-thing at once. Every moment of the last few years is there and I'm remembering them for the first time."

"It's fine. Take your time, dear." Gam Gam patted her on the shoulder and took the chance to slide a scarf around Izra's neck. The woman seemed not to notice for a few moments, but when she did, she looked over gratefully.

"How does someone fake living for thousands of years?" Mina asked, aiming her attention at the others in case Izra couldn't answer yet.

But Izra shook her head, focus returning. "I don't think he is. I think he's two hundred at most." Her fingers played with one end of the scarf, weaving it between her fingers. The action seemed to help settle her. "He's been needing more vitamancers every few years. It seems exponential, but I couldn't imagine he would need so few after thousands of years."

"What do you mean need so few?" Emil asked. "What does he need vitamancers for?"

She looked her brother steadily in the eyes and took a calming breath. "He's using us to heal his aging."

"He's healing *old age*?" Gam Gam asked.

"Only temporarily," Izra added. "It's why he needs constant healing and why he keeps needing more. His aging tries to catch up and he needs stronger power to stave it off."

"This can't last forever," Gam Gam said. "He must know that he'll run out of vitamancy eventually."

Izra focused on her memories for a few moments before she spoke again. "I think he plans to use a stone to give him true eternal life. He only has to last until he can use it, but I don't understand why he can't."

"The Wishing Stone!" Mina chimed in, then scrunched her eyebrows in confusion. "But I don't get it. I thought that captain said it was useless."

"It is," Gam Gam said, "while it's charging. He only needs to live long enough to make the wish, then he won't need the vitamancers anymore." Gam Gam stared off into the distance, then snapped her head back. "It's time to go. We need to leave now."

Gam Gam spun around and pulled a few bugs from her pouch. They came to life in her palm. Emil helped his sister stand, but she pushed him away once she was sure on her feet.

"We can't," Mina said.

Creases furrowed Gam Gam's brow as she looked back. "Mina, we've done what we could. We can help the others later."

"What if we never get another chance, Gam Gam? We must do something while we can."

"I can't lose you, Mina."

"You won't," Mina promised. "I know what to do. I can save them far faster than it took for Izra. Emil and Izra can help lead them out of the palace while the guards are distracted and—"

"The guards aren't distracted anymore," Gam Gam said. "We've run out of time."

Mina dropped her head, but her fists clenched to either side. Her modified memory flashed in her mind and she grew angrier. "I don't care, Gam Gam. No one should live this way."

"I can't leave them either," Izra said. "Not after knowing what they're going through. I wouldn't sleep at night."

"I'm not leaving my sister's side. Or Mina's," Emil declared.

Gam Gam looked them over, then, resigned, looked away. "It will be dangerous."

"I know," Mina said and the siblings nodded. "But you taught me that no matter how dangerous it is, you shouldn't turn your back on others. You risked your life to save mine. I want to return the favor for others."

Gam Gam nodded resolutely and pulled Mina into an embrace. "I am so proud of you, sweetie, and I know your father would be too."

Mina's heart thundered and filled with love and she couldn't help but smile. "Thank you, Gam Gam."

"It will be some time before the guards think to check the servant's quarters, so you have time to work. Emil, start scouting for pathways out of here while Izra helps them through the shock. My net of bugs will be watching and will warn you of coming guards. Start a trail out of here and save whoever you can."

Everyone nodded. "What are you going to do, Gam Gam?" Mina asked.

"I need to find Nugget first and hopefully I can find a few dead bodies to act as a distraction." Gam Gam smiled. "I'll be back as soon as I can, but don't worry about me. The bugs will be watching." Dozens of beetles and bees, roaches and centipedes spilled from her pouch to the floor. Izra stepped back, surprised and disgusted.

Mina nodded, but her heart clenched in her chest. It felt like a goodbye and she hated the idea she wouldn't see Gam Gam again. Instead, she said, "I'll do my best, Gam Gam."

"I know you will, dear."

They hugged and Gam Gam left.

Gam Gam sighed as she strode down the halls. She hated lying to Mina, especially in this way. But she had no choice. She stepped around the corner and Nugget hopped out beside her. Maybe it was her imagination or maybe her personal feelings crossed over the bond to her familiar. Either way, Nugget seemed especially feisty. "Did you get what I need?" Gam Gam asked.

Nugget clacked his teeth affirmatively and she confirmed as they turned the last hall to the antechamber of the throne room. A dozen undead stood in front of the doors, including Sloughy and Gerald.

Gam Gam stopped before the last of her forces, surveying the three guards tied up and stripped down, their armor now adorning undead of similar sizes. The necromancer nodded approvingly and stopped at one unarmored undead, just the right size. "Here, try this on," she said as she passed it some clothing she had grabbed from Izra's room. "Everyone else, make sure no one enters, understood?"

The undead nodded.

"Everyone ready?"

Again, they nodded. Gam Gam took a deep breath and wondered if she was ready. The necromancer pushed open the doors to the empty antechamber and strode in. To one side, a few seats were pushed against the wall for those waiting for an audience. Gam Gam found the most comfortable one and sat down. From her purse she withdrew her current project, a hat with a beautiful blend of browns and oranges that reminded her of autumn. Autumn was Gam Gam's favorite time of the year. The smell of leaves and the feel of the cold air on her skin. The warmth of her knitwear as she pulled the most comfortable garments out to stave off the chill. This hat was going to be a warm one and she had hoped to give it to Mina.

Mina reminded her of autumn too. It was when they had first met after all. It was when she had become the most important person in Gam Gam's life.

She hoped Mina would forgive her.

10

The great red doors creaked open at the touch of two brainwashed servants. The emperor and his retinue of thirty-two vitamancers stepped into the antechamber and came to a sudden halt at the sight of an elderly woman knitting in one of the chairs.

Knit two, purl two. Knit two, purl two.

Gam Gam sighed; she had hoped to finish the hat too. Now it would have to wait. She wrapped the needles within the project and slid it into her purse before looking up at the emperor. She could see it in his eyes, the annoyance that she didn't grovel at his feet. But there was intrigue there as well, even caution.

"I hope you don't mind," she said, leaning back in the chair. The cushion was very comfortable and the back provided more lumbar support than she would have expected. "I didn't want to interrupt anything, so I didn't knock."

The emperor smiled and walked steadily to the center of the antechamber, refusing to look her way. With a gesture, the vitamancers spread out, all focusing on him singularly.

"It is no trouble. I was beginning to worry you had declined my hospitality and left."

"Hospitality?" Gam Gam quirked her eyebrow. "I would hardly call a knife and a dungeon such."

"Ah, but the knife was to be quick and the dungeon stay short." He turned slowly, icy eyes staring at her. Gam Gam didn't shift. "But I think it's time for that to change. Where is my girl?"

"If it is Mina you speak of, she has a name and she is not your property."

"Not yet."

"Not ever if I have a say." Gam Gam pushed herself up from the chair with a groan. "I can see why you don't care for growing older." It was faint, but for a moment his eyes widened. His smile thinned. Gam Gam smiled innocently. "I've had this ache in my left knee for almost six years now. The cold causes it to flare like crazy. A vitamancer can soothe it for a week, then it's back to the way it was. The price of growing old, I suppose. It's not fun, but I like to think it's better to face what you fear than to run away from it. Death comes for us all some day."

"Not for me," the emperor growled.

"You're more optimistic than I am."

"If you won't tell me where to find the girl, then I'll just take what I need." The emperor took a step forward and Gam Gam felt his presence bash into her mind. Where Mina's touch was feather-light, the emperor's was a blow to crack open her skull. There was no subtlety and no defense. Not for someone without neuromantic powers.

Luckily, Gam Gam had a friend instead.

The emperor's presence disappeared a moment after it slammed into her and Gam Gam's blurry vision returned to her. She had stumbled back from the assault and now one hand propped her up against the wall while she breathed heavily. The emperor wrestled on the floor with one of his vitamancers—or rather, a certain undead woman who looked alive enough to pretend to be one. She had hidden by the door and joined the crowd as the others had come out.

The emperor was a man in his prime thanks to the vitamancers, however, and the woman's muscles had begun rotting away. He broke free from her grasp and kicked the woman to the side. Gaining his feet, the emperor stomped on the slower undead. Gam Gam looked away from the most gruesome of the effects but felt the tether snap under his assault.

Disheveled and furious, the emperor spun on her. "You think little tricks like this will stop me?" he roared. "I don't think I will kill you, *Gam Gam*." He sneered as he mocked the name. "No, I think I'll keep you alive long enough to let Mina do the honors. Oh, and I'll return her memories long enough to watch you die and know she was the reason. I can destroy your life and hers. I can take away everything you love before you die."

"You are already trying to do that," Gam Gam said, keeping her voice calm as her breath returned to her. She stood a little straighter, but the ache in her knee sent flames racing up her leg. "I have come to ask you to rethink your plans. Leave Mina alone and we shall leave in peace. We will leave your empire entirely."

"My empire knows no bounds! I have no need to negotiate with you. She *will* be mine, regardless of your desires."

"Perhaps," Gam Gam said. "But if conflict is had, there is a chance you do not leave this room alive. Would you risk hundreds of years of work on that?"

"Hundreds?" His eyes narrowed and one hand moved to his pocket. Gam Gam smiled. That would be where the Wishing Stone sat, she was sure. The emperor glared. "That girl," he growled. "She somehow found my memories."

"Yes," Gam Gam lied. Better he thought she'd found out during their encounter than wonder what Mina was up to now.

Then a calm came over the emperor and he smiled. "What is a necromancer without corpses?" He glanced around the room, then back at her. "It seems just an old lady. You knowing my secret changes nothing. Your army of undead was destroyed in the courtyard and you will not have had the time to gather more. You're bluffing and I—"

The emperor coughed. He stared at his hand, brow furrowed with more wrinkles than it had once had. The knuckles swelled on his shaking hand and soon spots formed on his exposed skin. His eyes darted to his thirty-two precious vitamancers. They slapped and swatted and tried to regain concentration only to be thwarted by another swarming attack of roaches, hornets, and beetles. The constant healing had shifted to a stuttering of healing and already the emperor's age shone through.

"I see your pests are for more than spying!" he croaked, pointing a shriveled finger accusingly at Gam Gam. When the mental attack came, it was weaker than before but no less overpowering. Nugget struck then, crashing into the emperor and knocking him off balance. The now old sovereign crashed to the ground in a yell, a servant rushing forward to pull the skeletal cat away. Nugget and the attendant fought a valiant battle as the emperor climbed to his hands and knees.

"Stop this and I'll let you go," the emperor groaned and looked up with watery eyes. "You and the girl both."

Gam Gam took in the sad sight of the emperor and almost stopped the attack. "I can't," she said. "Your word means nothing now. If you gain your—"

His presence smashed into her once more. Stronger than she would have expected in his state. Gam Gam gasped as her mental defenses were obliterated again. She felt the floor rush up to meet her, felt something crack and heard herself yell out. But overwhelmingly, one word rang through her mind.

Necromancy.

Memories flooded her. Classes in the mage's academy, Nugget's first steps as her familiar, the cleansing of Sir Gibblet's spirit, and the raising of Sloughy and Gerald. She clung to each memory as the emperor tore them from her skull. It was as if they were greased for her, slipping through her fingers every time.

The emperor's wrinkles deepened; his eyes sank. Every bone stood evident against his skin. She needed to hold on a little longer. It didn't matter what memories she lost if she could just hold out a little longer.

The clatter of cat bones rang through the hall when Nugget's spirit left. A bloodied attendant stooped next to the emperor and offered a hand. The emperor took it and as he stood, his wrinkles disappeared. The flesh grew healthier, his hair thicker. Gam Gam stared up in horror, tears falling from her eyes.

"Stop," Gam Gam begged the pale vitamancers. But they did not, pushing hard to heal the damage Gam Gam had caused. She had failed.

"They will not stop," the emperor spoke, the strength returning to his voice. "They *cannot* stop."

"I'm sorry, Mina," she mumbled.

The emperor stepped up to her and crouched. "You won't have to be sorry for much longer." The emperor placed a hand on Gam Gam's head and twisted so they stared into each other's eyes. "I've changed my mind; I'd rather be done with you sooner rather than later. But don't worry. You'll still be alive for Mina to kill."

The emperor's presence sliced into Gam Gam like a searing blade. The old woman screamed as the heat intensified, like having her mind scraped over a bed of coals. She felt everything he did, every bit of her mind being slowly shorn away. To be made into something less than the brainwashed. She felt everything she had ever done in life slip away, everything she had ever been disappearing. The emperor saved Mina for last, but even she was burned away in the end.

She watched the emperor's eyes burning with fury as the last of her mind died and she wondered if that was a new wrinkle in the corner of his eye.

11

Mina stood in a hallway of death. Corpses lay strewn across the hall, fallen from where their necromantic ties had been snapped. The skeletons in pieces, their bones scattered across the floor. A half-dozen soldiers were bound and gagged and shoved to the side unceremoniously. Mina ignored it all as tears fell down her face.

She had saved the servants, some forty of them, by clearing their minds. Understanding what had happened made the process so quick. Izra led them through the halls and out the side doors, the guards presuming them to be on some errand for the emperor.

But Mina had worried about Gam Gam when she had not returned. Fear had clutched her heart and she had known with sudden clarity where Gam Gam had gone. The still bugs lying in the hallway had sent her panicking and she had raced heedlessly to the throne room.

She was too late. Too late to stop the emperor. Too late to save Gam Gam. Her chest had been carved open from the pain within and only shock had saved her from screaming.

Grief could paralyze if you let it. Mina had recognized that before; it had consumed her fully in the times after her father's second death. Mina bit her lip hard, sending pain piercing down her jaw. Blood pooled in her mouth and her breathing slowed. She couldn't let it paralyze her now. She peered through the crack in the door and let anger fill her heart.

"What happened?" the emperor croaked as he examined a collapsed vitamancer.

Mina had happened, in that moment when she though there was still a chance to save Gam Gam. A wild lashing of her power, a reflex to stop the emperor. She had used the same coating as the emperor had in his mind control, but she'd targeted everything. The vitamancer was truly mindless, her power severed from healing the emperor. It hadn't been enough. He had finished whatever he'd done to Gam Gam before he'd even realized what happened. But now, his legs grew unsteady beneath him. Wrinkles slowly returned along his face. The healing had been weakened. Maybe Mina still had a chance to save the necromancer.

The emperor growled, then flung an arm at another healer. "Get me the others. *Now*! I need all the healing I can get."

Mina didn't let him make it more than a few steps. The man fell to the ground in a waking coma, every memory blocked off. The emperor looked up, startled, as Mina strode into the room. His smile chilled her, but she knew it was only a facade. He felt real fear and Mina would make sure it would never stop.

"My girl, you have returned to me." The emperor opened his arms in a welcoming gesture. Mina ignored him, glancing at Gam Gam prone on the ground. Her eyes stared blankly ahead. "That pain you feel," he added in a hoarse whisper. "I can take it all away. You don't have to—"

"I'll kill you." Mina's hands clenched at her side until they hurt. She trembled even more as the words fell from her lips. "I'll kill you!" she screamed.

The emperor only smiled. "Is that what you learned from your precious Gam Gam?" He stepped forward. "To be a killer? A murderer?"

Mina's breath hitched and her body shook. She looked away from the emperor and watched Gam Gam again. The slow rise and fall of her breaths. Perhaps it would have been better had the old woman died rather than whatever the emperor had done to her. The thought brought more tears and she wrapped herself in her arms.

"No." Mina gasped the word and sobbed.

The emperor stepped closer, his eyes shining. "It can be hard to look someone in the eyes and take their life," he said. "It has broken many strong men and you are but a young girl."

"No." Mina rubbed at her eyes and looked back at the emperor, meeting his gaze. "She taught me to value both the living and the dead. Even those I hate, even those who deserve it. I will not kill you."

"That's right, my girl." He stepped an arm's length away and Mina trembled beneath his eyes. He reached out a single, withering hand. "You are far too kind to kill. Far too kind for this pain you are feeling. Let me free you."

Mina jerked away from his touch, then squared her shoulders and took in a steadying breath. Holding his gaze was hard, harder than anything else she had ever done. "Fix what you did to Gam Gam."

The emperor's eyebrows rose and his smile wavered. "No."

"I will go with you freely if you fix what you've done."

"I cannot."

A flash of neuromantic power whipped out and struck the nearest vitamancer. Mina delved into the deepest reaches of his mind and smothered his false memories. In an instant, she was back within herself and the man collapsed. The emperor's eyes widened as he felt the loss of healing power flowing into him.

"You will try," Mina said.

"You fool!" the emperor hissed and reached for her. Mina stepped out of his reach. The man aged before her eyes, hair thinning and teeth yellowing. "I cannot! What I did is permanent!"

"If you save her, I will leave these healers with you until you die."

"I will not die! I cannot die!" The emperor stepped forward and his shaking legs gave out. He fell to the floor with a grunt and hateful eyes stared up at Mina. "I am *eternal*!" The emperor's mind slammed into hers with the force of a blow to her chest. The air fled from her lungs and she fell backward to the floor. The emperor's mental touch drilled into her skull and she screamed.

The Eternal Emperor stood at the beach of Mina's mind and laughed, victorious. Once she was his, it would only be a matter of bringing the healers back to heel. He would live long enough for the others to come. It had been a close call, but he was saved now.

He stepped into the pool and dove through the blackness to the mind. Its horrible flare of lights nearly blinded him as he reached out. A human mind was chaos and he was order. They should act simply, without so many hindering thoughts. He channeled his neuromancy and smiled.

The power fled him as he was snapped backward and up. He flew out of the pond of Mina's memory and was slammed to the ground. He grunted but was on his feet in moments. The bearings of this world did not work the same as the physical, but he had felt the touch like it'd been real. He looked up to see the girl stood in front of him.

"Impossible," he muttered. In hundreds of years, he had never figured out how to enter his own mind.

"This is *my* mind!" she shouted and then grew in size. Neuromancy flowed around her, forming many tendrils that snaked out. "Not your plaything!"

"Out of my way, girl! You're only making this more painful."

"My name is Mina." She coalesced her neuromancy into a gel. The emperor stepped back, eyes wide. How had she learned that trick? That was his! That was—

She threw it and the emperor screamed as the defensive neuromancy ate away at his presence. The gel dissolved his mental form, limbs fading into nothing beneath its onslaught. The pain lancing through the tether to his body was immense, like a hammer smashing at his skull. He fled.

The emperor collapsed in a heap, coughing and holding his head. Tears flowed from his eyes, but Mina felt no sympathy. She rose and stared at the pitiful old man. "Save Gam Gam."

"I *can't*," he croaked. Mina pressed a hand to the old man's head. Then she delved into the emperor's mind.

Gam Gam.

It had been a risk; she had only been able to reach her own mind when she'd followed the emperor's tether. That meant the emperor could do the same. But he was weakened from her attack and she needed answers.

Tendrils swept out across the memories that floated up, scanning them for the precise moment she needed. As they brushed each petal, flashes of the emperor's life burst into Mina's mind.

Mikyal lay strapped to a table as the emperor searched his mind. There he found the dismantled memories and pieced enough together to learn of a neuromancer and an old necromancer called Gam Gam, who had helped her.

An adviser spoke of Gam Gam, a graduate from the mage's academy with exceptional marks and moderate ability. She had often met with acquaintances at an establishment called the Dripping Bucket, making friends with the local ruffians.

A dozen locals drugged and unconscious lay strapped to tables. They had been brought in secretly and now the emperor searched their minds for any information on this Gam Gam. Mina recognized Clyde; he had not even known it had happened. It was within his mind that the emperor learned of Gam Gam's desire for the Wishing Stone. He smiled as joy flickered through the tendril. The bait has been found.

A soldier sat in a chair as the emperor reworked his mind. He had lost his brother a few weeks prior and had personally buried him. The emperor shifted his story and gave him motivation to find a necromancer, particularly one known to frequent the Dripping Bucket. He added a memory of a map and a great treasure. Then the soldier was left to his own accord and acted on his new memories. The emperor had only one more thing he had to do to complete the trap. From his pocket, he pulled the Wishing Stone.

The emperor had nearly died at the hands of a common woman. She had discovered his secret. Anger boiled as he felt the last twinges of the weakness of old age. He would plan better in the future, have more healers. He couldn't risk anything when he was so close to his goal. But treachery must be punished and his mood got the better of him. He thrust his mind into the feeble old woman's head and destroyed it. Not like his puppets. Here he ate away at the branches and the memories. He shredded the mind into pieces and seeped a poisonous rot deep within. She became a living corpse, a mockery of those she had raised herself.

Mina pulled back, gasping and trembling. Her hate dissipated beneath the overwhelming grief. She had felt everything the emperor had done, every moment he had spent tearing apart Gam Gam's mind.

"You understand now, yes?" The emperor pushed himself up and glared at her. "No vitamancy can save her. Nothing can repair her mind. But save my life and I can take that pain away. You will never have to feel this way again."

Mina trembled beneath the weight of his words. In that moment, she would have given almost anything to never feel that pain again. The incredible ache in her chest, like a claw rending her open. She felt worn out, like an over-stretched sweater. She pressed her palms into her eyes as more tears came. Gam Gam was lost to her and it hurt.

Mina rubbed at her tears as she turned. "I can't save you," she told the emperor.

"You can," he urged. "You can wake the healers. With their help, I will return to full power. Then you can be free."

Mina reached out to a healer, her presence brushing against theirs. Mina looked away from the emperor as more tears came. "But I can take away your pain."

Another healer dropped into a waking coma, their vita-mantic healing ceasing in an instant.

"No!" the emperor roared, but his voice cracked. He fell into a fit of coughing as his hair turned gray and his skin sagged from his bones. Mina clenched her eyes shut as the emperor groaned, his face transforming into a skeletal echo of what it had once been. She cried as she listened to the wordless croaks and the cracking of weakened bones. Then there were only her own sobs and she sat there long after, afraid to move.

When, finally, her eyes opened, where once the Eternal Emperor had been, there were only dust and bone and cloth. His skin had turned to parchment and disintegrat-ed with the lightest breeze. His bones had yellowed and cracked. His blood had dried to flakes. He was nothing but a dried husk. The Eternal Emperor had died.

"By the gods!" Mina spun and saw a soldier standing in the doorway. Behind him, the bound soldiers were being freed by another. "The Eternal Emperor is dead! The empire has fallen!"

The other guards stared with astonished awe and Mina stared back, afraid a single move would bring them bearing down upon her. She waited to be arrested or killed outright. She was far too exhausted to prevent either, far too numb to care. Mina's heart clung to Gam Gam's and hers was gone.

Then the soldiers spun away and scattered down the halls, yelling the news. Mina breathed out heavily and it turned into a quiet sob. She crawled to Gam Gam and placed the old woman's head in her lap. She stroked the gray curls and whispered, "Gam Gam? Are you there?" Gam Gam's eyes stared straight ahead, focusing only on what was directly in front of her. She made no attempts to speak. Mina wept. "I'm so sorry, Gam Gam."

She looked at the mindless healers, growing pale as they strained to heal the corpse in the center of the antechamber. She wanted to yell at them to leave but knew they wouldn't listen. She wanted to save them from their pain but didn't know if she had the strength. She ignored them, left them for someone else to help. But when she looked into Gam Gam's eyes, she knew there was no one else. She remembered a night so long ago when Gam Gam had pushed herself to collapse to save a little girl. Mina lowered her head to Gam Gam and held her. Then she placed the old woman's purse beneath her head to act as a pillow and began her work.

She started with those collapsed on the ground. She scoured the emperor's touch from their minds and clouded his false memories. They awoke screaming, each and every one. Mina held them until they calmed enough for her to tell them the emperor was dead and they were free. Every one of them shed tears. Every one of them laughed with joy. Mina could not echo their happiness.

Chaos streamed through the halls outside the antechamber. Various heads poked inside, but none confronted Mina. She was surprised when two arrivals stayed. She was more surprised when one of them talked.

"What happened?" Emil asked. Mina started, her vision too fuzzy from exhaustion.

Izra was at her side, steadying her. "We heard shouts of the emperor dying," she said as she rubbed Mina's back. Her warmth and vitamancy revitalized Mina and she finished her work with the last of the healers, then told both the healer and Izra the truth.

"The emperor is dead. You are now free."

"Good," Emil muttered.

Izra walked over to Gam Gam and knelt beside her, running her hands over her body. "She's alive," she said. "And awake, but I don't sense anything wrong with her."

Mina shook her head as she knelt on the other side. "It is her mind that is the problem. An attack from the emperor."

Izra held her hands to Gam Gam's temples and Mina could smell dirt in the air. Then she sighed and dropped her hands. "I don't think there's anything I can do."

Emil stared and Mina could see the tears forming in his eyes. His face contorted with anger and his knuckles grew white as he clenched his fists. He strode over to the emperor's corpse and spit on it. "Death isn't good enough for scum like you!" he roared as he delivered a kick. The remains exploded into a cloud of dust. Emil coughed violently and between the coughs, he choked out words of terror. "Oh gods! I think I inhaled some. I'm going to vomit."

Mina did not watch the flailing boy. Instead, she watched as the emperor's skeletal hand rolled away from Emil's kick, clutching a brilliant stone between its fingers. As if the emperor had scrambled for one last desperate attempt to save his life. Instead of the white Mina had remembered, the stone danced with a hundred different colors. The Tree of Life stood out vibrantly among ever-shifting colors.

It pulsed with reds and blues, greens and yellows, pinks and purples. Every shade of every color swam through its depths, filling the antechamber with radiant light. A radiant light that had not existed before.

Emil paused his flailing to stare in wonder and Izra let out a gasp. Mina walked in a daze to where the hand clutched the stone and pulled it free, the dead fingers cracking and disintegrating in the process. A warmth flowed from the rock and filled her with the familiar energy of her magic.

"Is that the..." Izra said at the same time Emil said, "It wasn't that color before!"

I thought that captain said it was useless.

It is while it's charging.

"Charging," Mina mumbled, her heart pounding in her chest. Did this mean it had charged? Could it grant her wish? Her hands trembled as she rushed back to Gam Gam's side. She needed to try something. *Anything*. She closed her eyes as fear filled her. What if it didn't work? What if it was all a lie? What if—

A hand steadied her, soft on her arm. She opened her eyes to see Izra with a soft smile on her face. She nodded. Then Emil sat next to Mina, a hand on her shoulder. He smiled broadly and Mina returned it as her vision blurred once more. She ignored the welling tears and looked down at Gam Gam.

"I..." Mina's voice cracked and she hesitated. She took a deep breath and ran the words through her mind. She needed it to be perfect. Misspeaking could ruin the wish. She ran through her breathing exercises and when she spoke again, her voice was steady.

"I wish for the damage caused by the Eternal Emperor to be healed from Gam Gam's mind."

The stone shone blindingly bright.

Epilogue

Smoke painted the sky a steel gray. Fires bloomed and spread across the city like a rampant disease. Shouts rang through the streets and brawls broke out. Mostly, the people hid within their homes, away from the discordance of Capital City, considering what would come next, now that the Eternal Empire had fallen.

Mina looked out from a balcony high up in one of the palace towers. The remaining servants and guards had barricaded themselves within and waited out the city's answer. They had been more than happy to house Mina after she had saved them from the emperor's brainwashing. Every single servant and guard had been tainted and she had cleansed them all over the course of several hours. The emperor's sway would hold no longer.

So much had been held together by a single person. With his death, it had all fractured within moments. It had been an astoundingly quick fall. It had been entirely her fault. All the pain caused that day was because of the choices she had made. She had shattered the world. But pain was not always a bad thing. Her father had told her that sometimes a fever had to grow worse before it broke. Sometimes an emperor had to die so that others could live.

"What is going to happen now?" Mina asked.

"I don't know," Gam Gam said. Her needles clacked as she put the finishing touches on a beautiful hat. It reminded Mina of autumn, her favorite season. The season she had met the most important person in her life. "But it seems change is upon us. *Necessary* change. Hopefully good as well."

Nugget woke from his nap—Mina still wasn't sure if the skeletal cat needed them or if he just pretended—and stretched out at Gam Gam's feet. Then he clacked and glared out at the city, seemingly agreeing with Gam Gam.

"Anything's better than the empire." Clyde leaned against the wall, arms crossed. His anxiety had lessened greatly when Lyla's girlfriend, a were-hawk named Callie, had arrived to bring news. His family was safe at the Dripping Bucket. If time couldn't tear that cesspool down, Clyde said, nothing would. Lyla slept, her head cradled in Callie's lap. Post-battle naps were an apparent tradition for her and she had waited long enough.

"I agree," Izra said. She placed a hand on Mina's shoulder and smiled. "If the public had known what the emperor was truly like, I am sure every one of them would be happy to pay the price of freedom. It is thanks to you that so many people have their lives back, Mina. Not just the vitamancers and other attendants, but the whole world is free from his clutches." She pulled Mina into an embrace. "You're certainly my hero."

Emil shrugged and rolled his eyes. "I guess you're pretty cool when you want to be." Mina stuck her tongue out and they both laughed. Surprise struck her when Emil pulled her into a hug of his own. "Thank you, Mina. For everything."

Mina ran her fingers across the alabaster plaque in one hand. Raised against it was the picture of a man in his thirties reclining in a familiar rocking chair, a book in one hand. He wore an easy smile and looked out with kind eyes. Mina lifted her pair of rings to her lips as she whispered, "I'm finally free, Papa." Whatever came next, she would happily face it.

Nugget's Tenth Life

Adam Holcombe

BOUNTY
INK PRESS

bountyink.com

Nugget's Tenth Life

There is a saying among humans that a cat has nine lives, but this is not entirely accurate. See, it is simply that cats are notoriously skilled at *almost* dying. It is only by the ninth time that the dying tends to stick. This is especially true about Nugget the Cat, though he wasn't called this in his life. For the purpose of the following story, however, we will refer to him by this name.

🐱 🐱 🐱 🐱 🐱 🐱 🐱 🐱 🐱

Nugget was only a few days old the first time he almost died, at the hands of a young human boy, no older than three, who should not be blamed for this fact. Newly born—a traumatic experience for many, street cats being no exception—Nugget was weak, his eyes unable to open and view the world quite yet. The boy found him particularly cute, and while Nugget's mother was busy nursing his sister, the miniature human snatched the kitten and ran.

I am not sure how much you know of human children but at the age of three (or so), many of the furless are unable to care for small animals. Especially newborns. In the boy's clutches, Nugget wouldn't have lasted another twenty-four hours. And so, it was lucky for Nugget that mother cats tend to be overly protective, with his being no exception. After a swift scuffle, the boy ran to his own mother with tears and scratches and hard lessons learned, and Nugget was carried back home to the abandoned and leaky house Mother had found for their small family.

His second near-death was more exciting. A young cat on the prowl, Nugget chased his siblings, Sister and Brother, through the streets and across rooftops. The city was a large place, with many nooks and crannies just wide enough for a cat to fit through. The three cats found them all and explored them all. Not many other creatures could navigate this part of the city like them.

There is a game nearly universal among living beings. It is meant to give the thrill of danger, without the chance of it. To be chased, and to give chase. Some furless call it "Tag." The cats have no name for it, but they play it nonetheless. Sister was in the lead, Brother and Nugget chasing her up broken framing to a dilapidated roof. She ran for the plank that acted as a bridge between the two buildings. Little did she know that it had rotted through and fallen into the alley only hours before. She was trapped, cornered.

Nugget and Brother stalked forward, hackles raised, ready to leap in whichever direction Sister went. She hissed back, then looked at the gap. She ran. Sister had always been the strongest, the fastest, and oftentimes the smartest of the siblings. She hit the other side, claws grasping stone, and clambered up over the edge. She turned to her brothers and meowed, tail flipping back and forth happily.

Brother yowled and turned to race down the building, but Nugget was made of sterner stuff (that stuff being the brilliant stupidity of youthfulness). He followed Sister over the edge of the building. Where her claws had saved her from a fall, his failed. Nail bit stone and scraped. His mewls rang through the alley as he plummeted, bouncing off one ledge and then a wood post.

Had he hit the ground, he likely would have broken something. As it were, he hit a strange hairless man with a missing eye. They both clattered to the ground, one in a hiss, the other in a grunt. Then Nugget untangled himself and fled, bruised, but not beaten. He had a sister to catch.

The third time involved a rancid rat and a lot of vomit. More than you'd expect, and completely unnecessary to go into details about.

With the weight of a few years on his shoulders, Nugget matured. No longer did he spend all his days playing with his siblings, though that is not to say he didn't spend any time with them. He just had responsibilities now. Some of the other cats had grown old, they weren't as quick or nimble anymore. So, it was up to Nugget and his siblings to patrol their little area, to make sure no other animals tried to take over their territory. Their family numbered almost thirteen strong. Other street cats were jealous, not to mention the strange dumpster-diving animals that cared little for designated territories and wandered where they wanted.

The biggest threat came from the calicos, a large clan of multi-colored cats. They wanted Nugget's home for their own, and one night they intended to take it. Four calicos cornered Nugget with grand plans to weaken their enemy by one.

Nugget fought back fiercely, but the odds were against him. Claws dug into flesh, and teeth sunk into skin. Tufts of fur were torn free, and blood was spilled. Nugget tired and fell to the ground exhausted.

The calicos would have pounced and finished the fight if not for Sister and Brother jumping in just then. Wearied from their battle with Nugget, the calicos ran away with their tails between their legs. Nugget returned home, and though he healed, some scars remained to remind him of the danger of his enemies.

Nugget was slow in the days after the calicos' attack. His skin still burned, and his wounds still bled. Though he was healing and moving faster each day, he had misjudged his speed when a fishmonger's cleaver nearly took off his head. The blade nicked a piece of his ear right off, and in his shock, Nugget dropped his fishy prize and ran.

Sister found him, licking one paw and rubbing at his newly sore ear. She dropped the fish at his paws and purred as she rubbed against him. Together they sat and feasted on the fish. Had the blade been truer of aim, perhaps Nugget would have lost his head on that occasion. Instead, he lost only a bit of his ear.

It was a stormy day when Sister gave birth to a litter of two cats, a male and a female. Booming thunder drowned the squeals of the newborns, and lightning crackled in the sky, bringing daylight in through the windows for a moment at a time. Then there was a terrible explosion, and the roof blew open to the winds and the rain. The wooden beams burst into flames, which soon spread and coated the inside of their little home.

Nugget hurried the other cats out into the rain, away from the all-consuming fire. It was only as Sister reached the alley, mewling in panic, that Nugget noticed one kitten was missing. She couldn't leave the one for the other, and Nugget wouldn't let her risk both. He raced back into the flames himself.

The heat pressed in on his sides, accompanied by the sound of hair sizzling when the flames brushed too closely. The kitten was in the center room, lit by the orange glow of the disaster. He squealed as tiny legs kicked out, and with a crack of the final supports, the roof collapsed inward.

Nugget raced as fast as he could, grabbing the kitten in his mouth as stone and flaming wood rained down around them. The fire scorched his side, as he raced upwards, through the flames and to the roof. Rain whipped against his agitated wound, as he balanced along the frame of the house. The flames below threatened to burn him and his nephew up, so he had no choice. Nugget ran hard and leapt the gap between the two buildings. He crashed into the other roof, claws digging into the side. This time, they stuck true, and he pulled himself up.

His family mewled in the alley as the building collapsed in a heap of flames. At least until they noticed his approach from behind them. That was the first time Nugget saved his nephew's life, and it wouldn't be the last. He brought the kitten to his worried mother, then lay down in the pooling water to soothe the wound on his side.

Homeless, Nugget and his family scattered across the city the next day, looking for a new home to fit their needs. It was while crossing one particular road that a horse drawing a carriage nearly stepped on the black cat with heavy metal feet. Nugget scrambled away, though the tip of his tail had become a little flatter than it once had been.

A great wooden bridge spanned the river that bisected the city. To one side was the market, and to the other was Nugget's new home. During the Dry Days, the river was calm and clear. During the Wet Days, it pulsed with anger. Of course, it would be during the Wet Days when Nugget's nephew fell into the river.

A thousand planks made the bridge, and nine hundred and ninety-nine of them were fine that day. One had cracked earlier in the week, and no one in the city had fixed it yet. It was too small a gap for the hardened feet of humans to notice. But for a tiny kitten?

Nephew played with his sister, weaving between the feet of the people. One moment they were bouncing off each other and rolling around. The next, he was gone, and Niece mewled in alarm. Nephew had slipped through the crack between the planks and was clinging desperately to the dangling wood. Sister pulled her daughter from the gap and cried out, trying to reach her son.

Nugget rushed to her side, reaching one paw down in hopes that Nephew could cling to it. He scraped and clawed, but in the end, the piece of wood broke free, and Nephew plummeted to the roaring depths below.

Sister cried out, but Nugget wasted no time. He leapt from the bridge and dove after the lost kitten. Sister grabbed her daughter, and the two raced off, trying to keep pace along the riverbanks as the two water-logged cats fought to stay afloat.

Nugget paddled swiftly to his nephew's side just as the kitten's strength began to falter. He snatched the kitten up within his jaws and desperately strained his legs to reach the riverbank. Sister ran along the edge, meowing, but Nugget could barely see her. Exhaustion battered him as hard as the waves did.

It was a relief when his paws hit the first of the stones at the river's edge. Nugget climbed to the edge and dropped the tired kitten at Sister's paws. She snatched him up and they were safe at—

The river swelled, sweeping up the edge of the bank in a rush, and Nugget felt his feet slip out from under him. He meowed as his head went beneath the water, and the edge slipped from his grasp. Powerful currents tugged him downward and away from the riverbank as he struggled to gather his breath before being sucked back under.

Nugget's limbs paddled slower and slower until he had no more strength left. He was dragged down the river, unable to stay afloat, and when he hit the stone, darkness overtook him.

He had thought that was the end of him in the moments before he hit the rock. At least until he woke up coughing water out on the side of the riverbank. He pulled himself from a laundry basket on shaky limbs and looked over at a very wet old lady. She smiled down at him as relief washed across her face.

"Oh good," she said. "Are you okay? Oh—"

Nugget ran off as some energy returned and he left the old lady behind. That was the eighth and final time Nugget almost died.

Nugget's old home was not the only one to be destroyed in the fires that raged that night so long ago. Many other abandoned shelters were destroyed as well. That meant safety and a dry room was a rarity for street cats. The calicos didn't much care for their own accommodations, not when the black cats' new home looked so inviting.

The calicos attacked, not as a small group cornering a single cat like their first assault on Nugget. No, they came in full force. Before his family knew what had happened, calicos were storming the large living space, claws and teeth bared.

Sister pulled back, protecting her kittens and retreating. As did the elderly cats who were too old to defend their home. Nugget stayed behind with a few others, fighting them off tooth and nail. His brother was at his side as they pushed back the calicos' attack.

But they were too few, and the calicos too many. He fought viciously, making them pay for each step they took. But it was all they could do to stay alive, let alone win. Nugget knew a lost battle when he saw one. So, he ordered a retreat. He told Brother and the others to run, find Sister and the elders, and protect them. He would make the calicos pay, then follow.

Nugget attacked in a flurry, breaking through the calicos and providing his family with a chance to escape. Before he knew it he was surrounded, one against ten. Their leader stepped forward, and Nugget turned to face her, hackles raised. When she pounced, Nugget dove away, circling to bite at her tail. As he did, however, one of her underlings bit at his own. Nugget jumped away from the new attack and landed within the leader's range. She swiped her claws across his face, drawing deep gouges across one eye.

Nugget jumped back, only to be prodded forward again by the circle of calicos. Each maneuver away from the leader led him to be attacked by a follower, and each attack against the leader was too slow. Each moment that passed saw Nugget's life dripping away more and more. The calicos viciously played with him, slashing at his ribs, nipping at his ears, bleeding him, and bruising him until he collapsed, too tired to fight on.

The calico took pride in her kill, a pathetic, hollow victory achieved by nothing more than letting her minions do the hard work. It angered Nugget as she bent down to finish his life. Angered him enough to push him, just one step further. With every last bit of energy, he jumped up at the leader, teeth biting down hard on the calico's ear. He tore the skin free as she yowled in pain. The ring of cats hissed at him and rushed forward. He ran. Ignoring the pain, ignoring the attack and the other cats, he pushed his way to the edge of the room, and leapt through a window that had been broken since long before his family took up residence there.

A shard of glass sliced one leg as he crashed through into the alley outside. Calicos stared out after him, hissing as he slunk into the night. He was tired and drained. He didn't know where his family had fled to. So, he walked until he couldn't anymore, hoping to catch any scent of them out there somewhere. When it became too much, he curled up at the entrance to a street, and he laid his head down for the last time in his life.

The last thing he remembered was an old lady's voice saying, "Oh dear." Then Nugget died.

This is the tale of Nugget's tenth life.

The first thing Nugget remembered was the bright light. It had just been dark, but the sun flowed through great stained-glass windows and painted the room in a dozen colors. He tried to blink away the painful light and failed to do so.

Several furless stood around the room, with Nugget lying on an elevated table. He stood and two others cheered. An old lady stared down at him with a large smile.

"Oh good, you're back," she said as she fiddled with something in her hands. Then she held it up, a collar, with a metal tag jangling at one end. Nugget's hackles rose, but that didn't feel right. "If you don't like the name, we can always change it, but I thought 'Nugget' fit well. Don't you think? You can call me Gam Gam."

She wanted to chain him as some sort of pet. He would never be restrained by the furless, enslaved to be some fat, lazy thing. He preferred freedom, he preferred his family. She brought her hand forward, and Nugget nipped at it. Then he hissed. Then he hissed again. No noise released. He meowed, he yowled, he cried out. Nothing, nothing, nothing. The other furless were yelling at Gam Gam about something, but Nugget ignored them.

He clawed at his face and felt little except the sensation of where his paws rubbed. He looked down and saw white.

They shouldn't be white. They should be... There should be fur! And there should be skin beneath that fur! But there was only bone where his legs should be.

Where was it? Where had this woman hidden his flesh? His blood should be leaking freely without it, but the table was unstained. Nugget prowled the table, sniffing, understanding the sensations that returned to him, but they felt wrong.

Gam Gam turned to him, cooing at him with a few noises that irked the cat. "If you just let me put it on you, I promise you'll like the collar."

Nugget mewled, his voice empty, and then he ran. Furless hands rushed forward to grab him, but he weaved between them, jumping from the table in a clatter. The old woman just watched as the other two chased, but they were too slow for him. All of Nugget's energy had returned to him, his wounds no longer bothered him, even with the lack of flesh on his legs, and so he sprinted through the halls of the great building in which he found himself.

The halls were filled with panicked furless, screeching and diving to one side as Nugget passed. They were cowards, not like the furless of the streets who would ignore a cat running by. Streets. Home. He needed to find his family. He needed to make sure they were safe.

Something pulled at him, though no line or net snagged him. Something within, and yet not a part of him. Something the cat didn't understand. He tugged back, feeling the old lady at the other end. It made no sense, she didn't collar him, didn't bind him with any ropes, yet she pulled on him all the same. Then the tug disappeared, and Nugget dove through a window into the courtyard beyond. He ran through lush gardens and into the streets of the city. He hadn't been here before, but elevated as it was, he recognized the bridge near his home.

Where his home had been.

The calicos would pay for what they did.

Where once he had stalked the streets of the city, ignored amongst the crowds of furless, Nugget now saw fear everywhere he went. They stared at him wide-eyed with anger and terror. They chased him with brooms and knives, and even the men in their metal clothing drew their sharp weapons as he approached. They hunted him down alleys like a monster, and Nugget fled.

He scrambled through a small crack into a building, escaping out of reach from the furless, and exiting out the other end before they could circle around. He stuck to the shadows, away from the terrified people, until he could hide beneath one end of the great bridge. The sounds of the furless and their strange foot coverings echoed down to him as he curled in the mud, catching the breath he didn't seem to be able to hold. Everything was strange, and he didn't understand.

Not until he stepped up to the water's edge and the cat that looked back at him wasn't the one he had known.

He couldn't blink, for he had no eyes. He couldn't speak, for he had no tongue. Nugget had been stripped of his fur and his flesh. Of his blood, and his life. Not just along his legs, but across his head and body. A skeleton stared back at him. The people feared him like a monster because he was one.

Nugget retreated and returned to his spot in the cool mud. A coolness he now recognized he didn't feel, but thought he felt. Everything was wrong because it wasn't real. Yet he saw, and he heard, and he recognized the feeling against his bones. He didn't understand, so instead he curled himself tight and hid away from a world that hated him as the sun dipped low in the sky.

His head perked up when the sound of a cat's screech echoed through the darkened streets of the city. A familiar cat's screech. He hurtled out from under the bridge, causing a man to jump and yell, spilling a crate of fish across the ground. Nugget ducked into unoccupied alleys, away from the furless, and chased after the cry.

Closer and closer, he approached his old home, now relinquished to the calicos. His hackles rose, or he imagined they did, at the mere thought of them. Of their cowardly leader, and even more cowardly followers. Closer and closer, he approached his sister's screech.

He pounced from the alley as four calicos ganged up on Sister and her kittens, now nearly fully grown. How long had Nugget been asleep? How long had it taken that woman to strip him of everything he was? It had to be longer than the day he first thought it was.

The calicos whirled as he dug claws into their hides. They yowled as he bit hard into the tail of one of them. Their own attacks glided off of Nugget's bones, never catching in what should have been flesh. They hissed and they retreated, terror at this new, foreign threat made them tuck their tails between their legs. Nugget hissed silently as they ran away.

Then he turned and found the kittens huddled behind Sister, shaking with fear. He looked at her and saw the defensiveness he had seen so many times before, except now it was focused on him instead of in defense of him. He meowed, and stepped closer, meaning to rub against her.

She hissed, and slapped his face with one claw, before leading her kittens away. Nugget watched as Sister disappeared around a corner, and once again, he lost his family. He laid down, then, and curled into a ball.

He was alone.

He was a monster.

"Oh good," the old woman huffed as she staggered up to Nugget. "I was worried you'd run off when I got too close."

Nugget had not moved in the time he had felt the woman's approach, nothing mattered to him any longer. He had no home to run to. Instead, he just turned his head away from the woman who had done this to him. She studied him for a moment, then with a great "oof" she dropped to the ground. The sudden movement jolted Nugget up and he whipped around to study the old woman who now sat on her rump.

"I'm getting a bit too old to sit on the ground these days." She sighed as she rubbed her hip, back propped against the alley wall. She watched Nugget for a moment, then pulled out a small ball of yarn, which she rolled to him. Nugget stared at it. "I heard cats like to play with yarn, I have plenty of it."

Nugget stared at her.

She sighed. "I'm not sure how much you understand," she said. "I hope it's everything. I suspect you understand that something strange has happened to you, and I'm afraid to say that it began with your death."

Gam Gam looked past Nugget, her gaze growing distant, her face becoming sad. Yet, here was the only person so far who hadn't kicked, yelled at, or run away from him. She was also the reason he was this way, so he curled back into a ball and made sure to not look at her.

"I'm training at the mage's academy to be a necromancer, that's where you woke up today," she continued. "I'm in the final year of my studies, and one of the lessons for my focus is raising a familiar. An undead creature that can act as a focus for a necromancer's abilities. Supposedly, it creates a stronger tie between the dead and the living, but you probably don't need to know the specifics."

She smiled at Nugget who continued to ignore her.

"I tried to save your life," she said. "I really wanted to, but you passed on even as I gathered you in my arms. You were in some sort of fight, weren't you? You had a lot of wounds." She fell silent for a long moment before continuing. "I did the next best thing I could, I raised you to be my familiar. Supposedly, it's common for a necromancer to crush their familiar into servitude, to wash away any personality or individualism, so they can act always as the necromancer sees fit. It's what they were demanding I do to you when you escaped. But I couldn't do that. It seems so horrible. What purpose is there to bring souls into this world if they can't be who they were?"

Something jangled in Gam Gam's hand, and Nugget glared back at her. She stared down at the collar in her hand.

"I want you to choose," she said. "You can come with me if you wish. It shouldn't be a hard life, I have a small bit of business out west, but that's about it. I can also return you to the dead if you dislike this form." She looked up and smiled. "There's a third option too, you can stay as you are, live your unlife as you wish, and I will let you be for as long as you want to be without me. You can live out your tenth life as you see fit. But either way, I have this as a gift for you."

She held out the collar to Nugget, who shifted his glare to the sign of servitude. The symbol of the lazy cats who sit by windows and eat what they're fed, acting as servants of cuteness to their masters. He would never stoop so low to serve a furless. Yet, she seemed to imply it wouldn't be servitude. Was it a trap?

"If you hate it," she said, "you can claw it right off. It doesn't have to stay on, but I think you might like it."

Nugget studied the woman. She was sincere, without a hint of deception, though Nugget wasn't sure what he could trust of his senses anymore. Still, he had little else to do now, so he held his head up and let her gleefully attach the collar.

"I know it's not perfect, but it's as close as I could get it." She pulled something from her pocket and held it in front of Nugget. The surface reflected his image like a still puddle. Nugget flinched back, but the skeletal cat no longer stared out. Instead, he saw himself. Perhaps younger, slightly different eyes. His ear was repaired, as was his tail when he flicked it behind him. He stared at himself, returned to flesh and fur, and jumped up with excitement.

"It's just an illusion," Gam Gam said as she passed a hand through the flesh in his neck with no resistance. "But it should let you be seen by others almost as you once were."

Nugget looked up, and when she smiled, he knew that she could understand him as well as he understood her. Gratitude.

She pet him, past the illusion, along his skull. She never flinched as her fingers ran down the bone. "I understand there is something you must finish here before you're ready to decide what you want to do," she said. "If you want help, you can let me know. Otherwise, I'll leave you to your business." Gam Gam grunted as she pulled herself up from the ground, using a nearby dumpster to help her stand. With a huff and a reddened face, she looked back down at the newly-fleshed Nugget.

"Do you remember when you were washed down the river, and I fished you from it? I will be there tomorrow again, to do my laundry. If you wish to stay with me, or you wish to move on past the Veil of Death, you can come find me. Our bond should lead the way. If you wish to stay here, there is no need to find me, I will leave you to your new life."

She smiled at Nugget, then waved farewell as she hobbled down the alley, one hand at her hip, and into the streets of the city. Night had fallen, and Nugget thought it was a great time for vengeance. But first, he needed to see his family once more, as he was now, so they wouldn't be afraid.

Despite a lack of flesh, Nugget's vision, smell, and hearing were all at their peak. He picked up Sister's trail in moments and traced it through the alleys and streets. Where fear had hounded him not long before, he was once more ignored by the furless. For all their apparent intelligence, a simple change had shifted their view of him so completely. He had to hope the same could be said for his family.

The trail ended at a dilapidated, one-story hut with a large hole in the roof. Eyes stared out at him from the shadows as he approached, studying him as if trying to recognize him, and when they failed to do so, huddling together for protection. Brother stood out front, Sister nearby with her kittens behind her. Their hackles were raised, and they were hissing.

Nugget was a stranger to them, even in this form. It was not close enough to what he had once looked like. Especially, without his recognizable wounds. He sat at the edge of the home's opening, a door long rotted to nothing, and watched his family prepare to defend themselves. He meowed, but of course, no sound left his lips. How was he to get them to understand who he was? He needed a way—

Sister stepped forward, sniffing the air. She meowed, then rushed forward. Nugget stepped back, but not fast enough, the cat reached him and began sniffing his collar. He carefully adjusted, making sure to not give away the illusion as she sniffed away. Then she backed up, cocked her head, and meowed a question.

Nugget's tail whipped back and forth in excitement as he silently meowed a response. He hadn't noticed it at first, but there was a scent he thought his mind had produced in its strange new state. A scent that had belonged wholly to himself. His collar smelled like it, and Sister recognized him.

Brother rushed forward, and Nugget cautiously backed away, swatting at him. He meowed again, and they both looked at him, heads cocked. Nugget lowered his tail, unable and unwilling to explain more, but they wagged their own, simply happy to see him again. Mother, old and frail these days, stepped forward with excitement in her tail. The kittens raced around and meowed joyfully. His family surrounded him and welcomed him home.

But it wasn't their true home. It wasn't where they belonged. Nugget worked his best to share his intentions with claw and head. They should wait for him to return so that he could bring them home.

Sister protested, begging him to stay, but as she grew close, Nugget bounded away. He had no choice, he had to make amends where once he failed. He had to get their home back.

It was the last thing he could do before leaving them forever. They wouldn't accept him if they knew the truth. *Couldn't* accept him. But that didn't matter, for they accepted him now, and they would accept him until it was time to leave.

Nugget raced off into the night, claws clacking along a cobblestone street.

An eerie wind blew through the alley when Nugget arrived at the entrance of his old home. The sounds of purring and meowing echoed through the building. A sturdy, water-tight roof. Strong, robust walls. A wonderful home. Dry from the rain and safe against the wind. Not like the hut his family currently cowered in. They wouldn't be there long.

He prowled around the building to find the small crack at the rear. He slid through, and weaved through a dusty room filled with rubbish, and up the central stairs to a large room on the second floor. He and his family had curled on the moth-eaten rug in comfort, huddling together when the nights grew cold, and looking out the windows at the stars and moon beyond. Now the calicos groomed themselves, stretching out in stolen comfort.

They hadn't noticed him at first, the silence of his approach only broken when his claws clacked against the wooden floor within the room. Ears twitched and heads turned to watch him form from out of the shadows, a golden gaze sweeping the room. They stood with anticipation, hissing threats. Excitement and a bloodthirsty desire to kill bubbling within each of them.

But it was especially hard to kill that which was already dead.

He leapt at the first calico, taking her by surprise as they rolled in a tumble. She bit and clawed at Nugget, but her natural weapons never found purchase in his false flesh.

Nugget's did, and they drew blood when he pulled them free. The calico yowled in pain, and the others joined the tussle.

He untangled himself from the first cat, and slipped between two others, weaving around their grasps and ducking under their swats. Their cowardly leader stood back and watched, injured ear twitching where Nugget had torn a chunk of it free. Nugget watched her even as he ducked around more attacks, even as he bit the tip of one calico's tail, and slashed at the ribs of another that grew too close. Their own attacks slid off his bones or slipped through the illusion harmlessly. They grew tired, and Nugget never wavered. Slowly, he bled the calicos even as they surrounded him and pushed him to a corner. It was nine on one, but this time he was winning.

They seemed to recognize it as well, no longer eager to put themselves in danger. As each calico approached, Nugget dove forward to strike and she would duck back out of the way. The leader stepped closer, anxiety twitching her ears as she watched for the killing blow.

She didn't know her family was filled with cowards. Nugget did, and it started at the top.

He clawed his collar free, the buckle clicking as it released. The metal tag clattered to the floor, and Nugget let out a mighty hiss (or what would have been one if he had the vocal cords for it). The calicos jumped back, hissing in return, or running to cower beneath furniture. The leader's tail stopped moving, her ears grew still. Every calico stared in horror at the undead cat. Nugget gave them no time to recover. He charged into the crowd, and they dove away, afraid of the skeletal monstrosity.

Only the leader didn't move. Her hackles raised, hissing and spitting, she pounced at him as he pounced at her, murderous intent flashing between them. The two crashed into each other with full force and rolled across the floor in a flurry of teeth and claws. Scratching, and biting at anything they could find, which proved more effective for Nugget and his skeletal body. For the second time, a ring of calicos watched their leader battle Nugget to the death, but now there would be a new ending.

Leader bit onto Nugget's bone and held, digging teeth into rib, but Nugget slashed across her side and she released her grip with a yowl. She jumped back, and Nugget chased. She swiped, and Nugget dipped around to attack her weakened side. Blood spilled from the calico's wounds even as Leader slammed into Nugget. The two rolled across the room, their claws a tangled mess. Then Nugget howled as Leader pulled his leg free, tearing it away from whatever supernatural force held it in place.

She jumped back, bones trailing in her wake, as she held the leg bone in her mouth. Nugget hobbled up onto three legs and glared. Leader was exhausted, panting, but Nugget was growing slower too. Was it because of Gam Gam? Or because of the lost leg? Would she be able to replace it?

Nugget stepped forward, then collapsed to the ground. Leader spit out the bone and yelled for her minions to attack. She wouldn't fall for the same trick again. The other calicos fell on Nugget, and he slashed at them all.

They were afraid of him, but still, they followed her. Which meant he only needed to remove that complication, and they would run. The skeletal cat burst from the mob of calicos, digging claws into the wood for stronger traction. Leader yowled as the bones slammed into her, dragging her to the edge of the room, and toward the window that Nugget had escaped through in a former life.

Nugget fought with fierce abandon, countering every one of Leader's useless attacks with one of his own that drew blood. The other calicos stayed back, cowardly, unwilling to face the demon that had come into their stolen home. Her attacks grew wilder, angrier, and easier to dodge. Nugget struck in a flurry, claw and teeth and tail slamming into her and pushing her to that window. She yowled just before Nugget tossed her out into the alley beyond. She yowled as she fell. She did not yowl after the wet smack against the alley floor.

Nugget turned, stumbling with the missing leg, and he hissed, drawing his claw across the wood. The other calicos understood, and they ran. Better to be alive and without home, in their opinions. He hobbled to his scattered bones, and sat, looking at them. He felt something within him, some strange pull so similar to when he first escaped from

Gam Gam. It seeped out from him and wrapped his loose bones in a strange, purple light. Then they shifted, and pulled back to him, arranging themselves into a workable leg, once more. His tail swished behind him as he stood to test it out, as perfect as—

He noticed her then, as he turned to retrieve his collar, standing in the shadows of the hallway beyond. Two golden eyes watched him closely, and his tail stopped moving. Then he sat and watched as Sister stepped into the room. Panic flooded Nugget's non-existent body, as his eyeless sockets looked to the collar and back to Sister. He needed to retrieve it and leave.

Sister traced his own gaze to the strip of fabric and sniffed the air. Nugget ran to the collar and snatched it up. He would have escaped out the window had her meow not stopped him. Not the hiss of fear from when they first saw each other, but a questioning meow. Nugget turned back to his sister and meowed silently, the collar dropping at his feet.

She hopped forward, licked his face, and then rubbed against him purring happily. Nugget leaned into Sister as she welcomed him, as she acknowledged what he was and didn't care. The kittens raced in next, running around Nugget excitedly, licking at his skull, and sliding against his ribs. Brother and Mother too. One by one his family returned, and one by one they welcomed him home. Nugget closed his empty eyes and felt their warm flesh flow across his cold bone, and he remembered what it had felt like in a previous life.

They spent the night there, curled together in one large group, Nugget at its heart. His family was safe, their home returned. When the sun rose, he didn't want to leave. But welcome or not, his presence would eventually cause trouble.

Sister woke with him, a soft purr asking him to stay. Nugget picked up his collar and set it down at Sister's feet. He rubbed his head against hers, and he meowed silently. This wasn't his home anymore; it was the home of the cat who had lived before him. This wasn't his family anymore; it was the family of his old life. But he would leave happy to know they were better off.

Nugget fled before the others rose, with Sister's howls chasing him through the streets.

"Hello dear," Gam Gam said as Nugget approached. "You seem to have lost your collar. Do you need a new one?"

Nugget sat and watched the woman as she pulled a dress from the river, then wrung out the excess water.

"Or have you made a different decision?" She paused in her wringing to look over. "Would you like to stay with me, Nugget?"

Nugget walked over to a recently cleaned knit blanket and curled up on it. Gam Gam reached down and scratched his skull, and Nugget slept peacefully.

Acknowledgements

Gam Gam and Mina wouldn't be here without the help of some magnificent people, including everyone who wanted to read more of their adventures. This book exists because of those of you who loved A Necromancer Called Gam Gam. Thank you so much, and I can't wait to write more!

First and foremost, thanks to my wife, Sarah, who has been by my side during my entire writing adventure, and who always believed I could make it this far. She is my first reader, my first editor, and my knitting expert. Anything wrong with the knitting is her fault entirely.

A special thanks to Dylan, a steadfast friend since middle school, and my first confidant after Sarah. I still remember you telling me "You could be a published author," without having read anything I wrote. Thanks for your undying belief that I could do it!

Gam Gam started as a D&D character I thought would be fun to play, back when I was a Forever DM (I've broken free!). Fortunately, I mentioned this before I got the chance to play her, and two incredibly special people bullied me into turning her into a story instead. Gam Gam wouldn't be here without the ruthless bullying of Connor and Krystle, so thank you for pushing me down this path.

To my beta readers, thank you for telling an incredibly nervous Adam that the story worked! Thank you Azshure, Chloe, Dylan, Joe, and Ribbon! Your insights were invaluable and helped make this a better book.

To my editors, who improved on everything I did, thank you so much. Taya for your commas and clarity and polishing of my words into something far better. And Isabelle for your close attention to detail to smooth the story out. And especially for being so excited for the story and being a constant cheerleader of my work! I can't wait to get you book 3.

A big shout out to those on the discord channels who constantly cheer me on! Your endless support have helped me become more consistent writer, and have created some wonderful friendships.

Endless thanks to those who made Gam Gam look better than I ever could have dreamed possible. I'm lucky to have an immensely talented friend like Kerstin to make my book look amazing every time. (Insert bear GIF.) To Virginia, your ability to compliment Kerstin's artwork with the layout is incredible. The cover for the first book deserves so much of Gam Gam's original success, it wouldn't be what it is without your help, and the sequel continues to be amazing!

To the many friends I've made through Twitter and Discord, thanks for always cheering me on and making me feel welcome among the indie book community.

And lastly, thank YOU for continuing your adventures with Gam Gam and Mina! I hope you enjoyed their next adventure, I'll keep writing this for as long as you want them!

Acknowledgements: Nugget's Tenth Life

Ever since A Necromancer Called Gam Gam, I've been thinking about how Nugget and Gam Gam meant, with every intention of creating a short story for them, just as I had Sir Gibblet and Gam Gam. I am so happy to have been able to do this for The Wishing Stone's release! It was a challenge to make a story about a cat that died interesting enough to not have everyone bail at his death. I hope you were able to stick around and enjoy the story! If not, I understand and I'm sorry!

First and foremost, thanks to my wife, Sarah, who has been by my side during my entire writing adventure, and who always believed I could make it this far. She is my first reader, my first editor, and my knitting expert. Anything wrong with the knitting is her fault entirely.

A special thanks to Dylan, a steadfast friend since middle school, and my first confidant after Sarah. I still remember you telling me "You could be a published author," without having read anything I wrote. Thanks for your undying belief that I could do it!

To my beta readers, thank you for checking out the early story and letting me know your thoughts! Thank you A.C ., Dylan, and Joe! Your insights were invaluable and helped make this a better book.

For my editor, Sue, thank you for improving upon the story and making Nugget's Tenth Life better than I ever could alone.

A big shout out to those on the discord channels who constantly cheer me on! Your endless support have helped me become more consistent writer, and have created some wonderful friendships.

To the many friends I've made through Twitter and Discord, thanks for always cheering me on and making me feel welcome among the indie book community.

And lastly, thank YOU for taking the chance to read this short story about a cat and his tenth life. I hope you enjoyed your time with Nugget!

About Author

Adam Holcombe daylights as a programmer and moon-lights as an author. After spending years toying with the idea of writing, he decided to commit and work toward releasing his first novel. Then Gam Gam got in the way, and now he's writing too many stories to count.

When he's not locking himself in a cold basement to type away, he can be found squishing his dog (but not too hard), squawking at his tortoise (but not too loudly), goofing off with his wife (in perfectly ordinary, non-weird ways), playing D&D with friends (I'm playing a character now!), or the usual chilling at home. He is a lover of books, board games, video games, and swords.

Mina and Gam Gam will return in the future, but until then keep your eyes out for the sci-fi novel, Bounty Inc, which will launch a series Adam is very excited to delve into.

Check out bountyink.com for future publishing news, and additional book content.

9 781960 544056